Nicole Moon
6616

ALSO BY CASSIE EDWARDS

Wind Walker
Night Wolf
Racing Moon
Storm Rider
Spirit Warrior
Fire Cloud
Midnight Falcon
Winter Raven
Sun Hawk
Thunder Heart
Silver Wing
Lone Eagle
Bold Wolf
Flaming Arrow
White Fire
Rolling Thunder
Wild Whispers
Wild Thunder
Wild Bliss
Wild Abandon
Wild Desire
Wild Splendor
Wild Embrace
Wild Rapture
Wild Ecstasy

PROUD EAGLE

❖❖❖❖❖

Cassie Edwards

A SIGNET BOOK

SIGNET
Published by New American Library, a division of
Penguin Group (USA) Inc., 375 Hudson Street,
New York, New York 10014, USA
Penguin Group (Canada), 10 Alcorn Avenue, Toronto,
Ontario M4V 3B2, Canada (a division of Pearson Penguin Canada Inc.)
Penguin Books Ltd., 80 Strand, London WC2R 0RL, England
Penguin Ireland, 25 St. Stephen's Green, Dublin 2,
Ireland (a division of Penguin Books Ltd.)
Penguin Group (Australia), 250 Camberwell Road, Camberwell, Victoria 3124,
Australia (a division of Pearson Australia Group Pty. Ltd.)
Penguin Books India Pvt. Ltd., 11 Community Centre, Panchsheel Park,
New Delhi - 110 017, India
Penguin Group (NZ), Cnr Airborne and Rosedale Roads, Albany,
Auckland 1310, New Zealand (a division of Pearson New Zealand Ltd.)
Penguin Books (South Africa) (Pty.) Ltd., 24 Sturdee Avenue,
Rosebank, Johannesburg 2196, South Africa

Penguin Books Ltd., Registered Offices:
80 Strand, London WC2R 0RL, England

First published by Signet, an imprint of New American Library,
a division of Penguin Group (USA) Inc.

ISBN 0-7394-4754-8

PUBLISHER'S NOTE
This is a work of fiction. Names, characters, places and incidents are either
the product of the author's imagination or are used fictitiously, and any resem-
blance to actual persons, living or dead, business establishments, events, or
locales is entirely coincidental.

The scanning, uploading, and distribution of this book via the Internet or via
any other means without the permission of the publisher is illegal and punish-
able by law. Please purchase only authorized electronic editions, and do not
participate in or encourage electronic piracy of copyrighted materials. Your
support of the author's rights is appreciated.

In admiration, I dedicate *Proud Eagle* to Genny Oster-tag. She gave her heart to her career as an editor at NAL/Signet and is now on her way to new horizons. Thank you, Genny, for your guidance as an editor, and I wish you the very best in all of your endeavors.

Always,
Cassie Edwards

As the crow flies with the wind, he does not tell of his flight.

Unlike man, he cannot tell who is evil and who is good.

He does not see with his eyes.

Nor does he hear with his ears.

But he understands with his heart.

His wishes are that all those that pass before him pass in peace.

As spring brings the winter, so death begins with birth.

This is only one step in the great circle of life.

The great crow's belief is if one must fight, he must fight without fear.

The pride of the evil man has blinded his eyes to the true meaning of life.

The crow is the lost one, but his words all must hear.

Let us all part in life, and not in death.

—GLENDA D. RUPPERT

Chapter One

Eagle Bay, Washington—Autumn 1880

The cloudy sky flickered with a crackling blue light as Chief Proud Eagle of the Makah Indians, White Owl Clan sat on his horse on a high hill, alone.

Wearing a laced elkskin shirt, breeches, and moccasins, he gripped his reins tightly. The hollow feeling welled within him as he looked down at a white man's three-storied mansion.

From the time this dwelling was built five winters ago, it had always looked out of place. The white lumber baron had brought his business from Seattle, near which he was known to have carelessly stripped vast parcels of land. Since he had arrived on Makah land, he had taken by treaty acres that had belonged to the Makah and he had built his home and lumber company on that land.

What made Proud Eagle angry was the carelessness in how he felled trees near Eagle Bay. Proud Eagle and his warriors were very careful about which

1

trees they chose to cut. The white lumber baron's practices had already caused problems. When it rained, water poured down through the gouges, creating deep grooves in the earth, and stripping land as it traveled close to Proud Eagle's village.

There had already been one major mud slide, which had claimed some Makah lives, among them kin of Proud Eagle. Proud Eagle was still fighting against his need for vengeance. He was a man of peace. But if it happened again, all hope for peace would be erased from his heart. He would be out for blood.

Eagle Bay was located in the narrow margin between ocean and forest. It was a place of paradise for his people, their beloved home, where they flourished.

The women cared for their gardens and gathered wild plants in the forest, while the men worked in the forest felling trees or fished from the rivers, tidal pools, and open sea for their food, as well as for trade with white people.

But unlike other Makah clans, his did not work to pull their existence from the sea. His people's lives centered around lumbering. Almost every aspect of the White Owl Clan's life depended on wood, which the Makah worked masterfully. An artist needed special tools like his whalebone chisel, and a beaver-tooth knife with a wooden whaler head haft to fashion objects of great spiritual power.

A movement below drew Proud Eagle's attention. A woman dressed in black left the house and walked toward a fenced-in area that he had learned was a recently established family cemetery. The lumber baron had been buried within the confines of the white picket fence.

Proud Eagle had never liked the man. He had proved himself to be cunning and aggressive in his dealings with the Makah, and Proud Eagle had never trusted him.

But just because he was dead, Proud Eagle did not think things would change. There was another man that Proud Eagle could only surmise was the baron's son or partner. What mattered most to Proud Eagle about this man was that he was just as shrewd as was the older man. Proud Eagle hoped to discover just what this man would do with the business and the estate.

It was certain that the road ahead would not be easy. He feared that the surviving partner would try to break treaties between the Makah and the United States government that had left the Makah in charge of vast stretches of forestland.

Proud Eagle would make sure that this did not happen.

He focused his attention on the woman in black. She wore a lacy veil on her hair, leaving her face exposed. He knew that she was grieving the loss of the lumber baron, for she went and knelt beside the fresh mound of dirt, her head bowed.

He could see her face well enough to discern that she was a stranger to this land. It puzzled him that he had never seen her before and wondered what could she have been to the man. Might she be the daughter of the deceased? Or was she related to the man who now was in charge of the estate?

Suddenly the wind picked up and whisked the veil from the woman's head, blowing it away over her shoulder. Proud Eagle's heart skipped a beat when he saw the thick, brilliant-red hair that fell down the woman's slender back to her waist.

She rose from the grave to chase the veil tumbling along the ground, close to the hill upon which Proud Eagle sat. He was able to see her face more clearly and was taken aback by her absolute beauty. He had never seen anyone as lovely, not even among his Makah women!

And she was tiny, so tiny he felt that if the wind became any more brisk it might lift her from the ground and take her along with it, as a feather might be blown away. Proud Eagle's curiosity was aroused. Who was she, and where did she come from?

Finally she caught the veil, but she didn't put it on. Instead, she held it at her side and walked slowly toward the house.

Needing to get back to his village, Proud Eagle swung his horse around and rode away. Tempted to look at the woman again, he glanced over his shoulder. The fiery-haired woman was looking up at him. He quickly averted his eyes from her and dug his heels into the flanks of his horse, sending him into a hard gallop toward his village.

Chapter Two

Billie Shaughnessy was surprised by the Indian on the horse. She knew that he had been watching her. Somehow, though, she did not feel threatened by his presence, regardless that her father had had problems with Chief Proud Eagle. The Makah were still protective of the land and trees that by treaty were her father's. And they certainly were not happy about her father establishing a lumber company so close to their village.

As she walked toward the mansion, she wondered if the man on the horse might be the Makah chief, Proud Eagle. On the occasions when her father returned to Seattle for brief visits with Billie and her mother, he had spoken about Proud Eagle with bitterness. It was the Indian chief who kept her father and his company at bay, watching to be sure that her father did not go farther than what the treaty allowed him to.

She could only surmise that he was here today to

see what might happen to the lumber company and land now that her father was dead.

Billie remembered her father's mentioning Proud Eagle's disarming charm. But he had not been able to budge her father's decisions about anything in regard to his lumber business.

If Chief Proud Eagle discovered who Billie was, he might try to use his legendary charm on her. She noticed how handsome he was, with his thick waist-length, raven-black hair that billowed in the breeze as he rode away, his midnight eyes, and his sculpted features. Billie knew that she must be on guard at all times against this man, who surely could win any woman that he wanted.

She guessed that the handsome chief was in his mid-twenties. She herself was almost thought a spinster at her age of twenty. She wondered what he was thinking about as he watched her.

"What am I doing?" Billie said harshly to herself, even as she looked again at the hill.

Walking again toward the mansion, she swore to herself now, as her eyes were drawn to her father's grave, that she would not allow the Makah chief to get away with anything. She was in charge of her father's business now, and she was her father's daughter in every respect.

She had been taught all aspects of lumbering when her father had his company just outside of Seattle. As early as age eight, she had gone with him into the forest and learned how to choose which trees were to be cut. Before he had moved his company to "better pickings"—as he had described the land that sat near Eagle Bay—she could stand up next to any man and best him at lumbering. She had been nicknamed a lumber*jane* by the men who worked with her father, mocking how the men were called lumber*jacks*.

When she stood in the tall shadow of the house, she stared up at it and was lost in thought again. She had been fifteen when her father had left Seattle. Neither Billie nor her mother had accompanied him.

Her mother, a socialite and owner of one of Seattle's most prestigious millinery shops, had refused to move to a place so isolated and wild.

Her mother's frail health was also a factor. Her heart had been weakened by a childhood disease, and she wanted to stay where she could have a doctor come quickly should she need one.

Although Billie was built like her mother, she was far from being frail. She had proved to be a strong child, and she wanted to go with her father, but had decided in the end to stay with her mother. Billie wanted to be able to take care of her if she should need help.

She knew if she had gone to visit her father at his new home, amid the towering trees and nature that she adored, she would have been too tempted to stay. Therefore she had never been to Eagle Bay, not until it was time to say farewell to her beloved father.

Now that she was there, Billie saw just how beautiful the mansion was and knew that he had built it in hopes of luring his wife and only child to live with him there. But that had never happened. Her mother would not budge from Seattle.

Everything in Billie's life had begun to change drastically six months ago when her mother's frailties had finally claimed her. She died suddenly of a heart attack.

Billie had barely gotten her mother's affairs in order, selling the millinery shop and the Seattle mansion, when she received the horrible news that her father had been injured on the job. His death had come quickly. She still was not certain how he had died, though—she had been told only that it happened while he was working with his men, felling trees.

Suddenly Billie was alone in the world. She had always hated being an only child, but now she realized how lonely it could truly be.

But she was a survivor. She was strong not only in body but also in mind. She would come through these trying times a stronger person.

She had left Seattle only last week, and she was now at her father's house, on her father's land. Soon she would figure out what she must do next. First, though, she had to cope with her grief.

She wiped the tears from her eyes and went into the house, only to come face-to-face with Roy Clawson, her father's partner.

Billie stiffened when he gave her his bucktoothed

smile. She had known him when the company was based in Seattle, and she despised this sweaty, bald, obese man whose pale gray eyes always seemed to be looking through her.

He used to stare at her with lust, but now he looked at her with a strange sort of contempt, surely borne of the belief that a woman could not take over a "man's job."

"Well, now, how's Billie Boy today?" Roy asked mockingly, causing Billie to frown.

He knew all about her and her family after being with her father for so long, and he knew why Billie had been given her name. Her father had wanted a boy, especially since her parents had been told that her mother wasn't strong enough to go through another pregnancy. So Billie had become that son.

She had been taught everything a son of Theodore Shaughnessy would have been taught. She grew to love not only lumbering but also horses, firearms, and the comfort of men's clothes. Her mother had tried to soften the effects by teaching Billie about owning a millinery shop, and how to dress the part of a "lady." Billie had to learn to play the dual roles.

"I do not appreciate being called Billie Boy," Billie said crisply. "Please remember that, Roy Clawson, and we'll get along a lot better."

"Yeah, sure, *Billie* Boy," Roy said, his eyes gleaming. "Or maybe now that it's just you and me, I'll call you Red. I've always admired your red hair—it fits your personality to a T."

Billie's jaw tightened. It was clear just what she had ahead of her. She had a fight on her hands as far as this man was concerned. He had been her father's partner for many years and had worked his way into the company that had at one time belonged solely to the Shaughnessys.

Until she could figure out a way to get rid of Roy Clawson, she would have to cope with the situation as best she could. She would study her father's finances and if he'd been as rich as she thought he was, she would try to buy Roy's portion of the business.

She was already wealthy, since she had sold the millinery shop and the Seattle home. But it would take more money than that to get rid of Roy for good. She could hardly stand to be near him, much less share a business with him.

"Roy, can we for at least for the moment forget our obvious contempt for one another?" Billie asked. "I plan to go over Father's books. I need to busy my mind. That's the only way I can get past my grieving."

"Fine," Roy said. He took a silver flask from his inside jacket pocket. "What'cha need? How can I help?"

He tipped the flask to his lips and swallowed a few sips of whiskey, then screwed the cap on the flask and returned it to his pocket.

"I want all of my father's journals and ledgers,

personal and otherwise," Billie said, draping her black veil over a chair in the foyer.

She headed toward her father's office, giving Roy a look over her shoulder as he followed. "And I want the combination to Father's safe," she said, lifting an eyebrow when she saw his eyes narrow at her request.

"Which . . ." Roy said, then quickly stopped himself. "I'm not certain where he kept everything. I ain't one to know numbers that well. Your pa was the educated one, so I trusted him to put the right figures in the books."

"Then take me to the safe. Maybe what I need is there," Billie said, entering the massive office.

She stopped and gazed slowly around her. It was a grand room, large, with tall ceilings. One whole wall was lined with expensively bound books. On the opposite wall was a wide stretch of windows that looked out past the yard and into the wonders of tall Norway pines. Past the pines stood a massive forest, with all kinds of trees.

The end wall housed a huge stone fireplace, now with cold ashes beneath the grate. Her father had always loved staring into the flames while going over his day's activities in his mind. She could almost see him sitting there now before a crackling fire, smoking a pipe, with his legs outstretched, his feet resting on a footstool, and a glass of port in his hand.

She remembered that when she was a child, her

father would come home smelling of wood and the forest, and she would sit close to him on the floor with her cat on her lap. She loved hugging him and inhaling those fresh, clean fragrances, which now would always remind her of her precious daddy.

Her gaze drifted toward the huge oak desk in the center of the room. She imagined him behind the desk, sitting in the sprawlingly large leather desk chair, a fat cigar in the corner of his mouth, his green eyes twinkling. In his younger years, he had been such a handsome red-headed Irishman. Even as an older man, he had a personality that could charm a snake!

She went on to the desk and gaped openly at the clutter. Journals, books, ledgers, cigar stubs piled high in a massive ashtray, and many other things that she couldn't identify were scattered and piled on the desk.

"There's the safe," Roy said, motioning toward the far wall behind the desk.

He went to the desk, opened a drawer, and pointed to several numbers written in ink on the inside. "That's the combination," he said. "Although your father was educated, he had trouble remembering the numbers to open the safe."

Billie gazed at the numbers, then at the journals and ledgers, then at Roy. "Thank you, Roy," she said tightly. "I think I have all I need here. You can leave. I've lots to do."

"Dismissing me, eh?" Roy said, his eyes again narrowing. "All right, I'm leaving. But remember this, Billie Boy—I am your partner now."

"Just please leave," Billie said, more and more annoyed by the crude man.

Roy glared at her and took another swallow from his flask. Then, laughing, he turned and left.

"Finally," Billie whispered.

Unlike her father, Billie was one never to forget anything. She memorized the combination to the safe, then took a pencil and scratched through the numbers inside the drawer, over and over again, until they were no longer legible. Roy might know the combination, but Billie doubted that any of the other lumberjacks did.

She sank to her knees before the safe, turned the dial according to the combination, then swung the door open wide and peered inside.

"There's hardly anything at all here," she whispered.

She took out a small ledger and set it aside on the desk, then thumbed through papers that had been stacked neatly beneath it. She saw nothing of importance there. She closed the safe and locked it again, then sat down at the desk.

With the smell of stale cigar smoke and sweat emanating from the chair, she opened the ledger. She studied the figures page by page, until she came to two places where pages had been torn out. Her brow furrowed as she examined the pages before and after those that had been removed. None of them made any sense. The figures posted there in ink most certainly didn't balance.

As she further studied the ledger figures, she kept glancing at the journals sitting on the desktop.

She recalled seeing one locked away in a drawer in her father's bedroom. Suddenly she wanted to read it. She could only surmise that it was filled with entries about her father's feelings toward family and his daily life.

Though she was weary, Billie went to her father's bedroom and took the book from the drawer. She sat down in a comfortable chair beside a window and opened the journal to page one. Immediately, tears filled her eyes, for the journal started when she was ten. He wrote about being with her that day, horseback riding where they could get a good view of Mount Rainier in the distance. She loved that mountain and the times alone with her father.

She read on through the pages, knowing that it would take days to finish it. But the journal contained her father's feelings about her and her mother and his love for the business that he had built from scratch. It inspired her not to let go of the past, but instead to follow in his footsteps. She would keep her father's dream alive.

She would begin tomorrow by becoming part of the crew, helping to fell trees. What a surprise it would be for the men, and especially Roy, that she had decided to stay.

She had gotten the feeling that Roy hoped she

would let him have full control of the business. No ladies worked with lumberjacks.

Well, she had a thing or two to show him. If the ledgers were correct, something was wrong, and she intended to search until she discovered exactly what it was. She wondered if Roy was the one who had removed those pages or if her father had.

In time, she would know. She would know everything there was to know about her father's business since he had left Seattle. She would find out all she needed to know about Roy, too.

She rose from the chair and set the journal aside. She had an announcement to make, not only to Roy but to the entire crew of lumberjacks. Suddenly she smiled mischievously.

She hurried to her bedroom and yanked off the black dress, then searched through her trunks for something more appropriate for the sort of life she would now be leading.

When she found a pair of trousers, she eagerly pulled them on.

"Watch out, Roy, here I come," she whispered as she pulled on her boots.

15

Chapter Three

Roy paced the floor at the large bunkhouse as the men sat watching him. Suddenly he stopped, placed his fists on his hips, and looked icily at one and then another of the crew.

"Men, I see trouble ahead," he said tightly. "I just know that Billie Boy will sell out so she can get back to her fancy living in Seattle. She wasted no time selling her mother's millinery shop after she died. Surely she has the same in mind for her father's lumber business. She's sure to discover that I no longer have any ownership of this lumber company because of my love of gambling. If she does, she'll give me the boot."

He cleared his throat nervously ran a hand across his gleaming head. "You all know that I still want what's best for the business. Who's to say who will buy her out and be in charge? Well, men, I say to those of you who want to save your jobs, side with me. I promise to ensure your jobs if you do."

"How?" Adam Sparks asked, his eyes narrowing

questioningly. "What'cha got on your mind? If she discovers that you don't have any control of the business, you'll be sent packing, that's for sure. I've seen you two together these past couple of days. There sure ain't no love lost between you."

"I'd like to remedy that, that's for sure," Roy said, snickering. "Ain't she a beaut? Who'd not want to have a night or two in her bed?"

"So that's part of the plan?" another man asked. "Getting her in bed first, controlling her second?"

"I'd like nothin' better'n that, but she cain't stand the sight of me. She sees me as a bald old coot, so I doubt she'd ever let me lay a hand on her," Roy said. "All's I'm concerned with is this company that we've all had a role in building since the early days."

"Then how are you going to do it?" another man asked.

"I've got to play it by ear for a while," Roy said. "I've got to see just what she has in mind."

"So you're sayin' that if she decides to sell out before you can get a plan together to stop her, we'll all be out of a job, or under the thumb of someone we don't know?" Earl Biggs grumbled.

"Yeah, something like that," Roy said sullenly. "For now, I've done enough to confuse the issue. I destroyed what records that I felt could prove I don't have any monetary ties to the business anymore. We'll see what else she comes up with."

"Well, hello there, gents," Billie said as she came into the bunkhouse.

Roy looked startled. He had to wonder if she had heard anything that had just been said.

He stepped away from her and stood with the other men, who had all stood up from their bunks.

"Hello, ma'am," the men said one by one.

She could see their eyes raking over her, as they studied her attire. Roy's color had faded with shock. She nodded toward him.

"Well, Roy, what do you think?" she asked, turning around, so that they could all see her outfit.

"I ain't never seen the like," said one of the men. "A lady in breeches?"

"Yes, and I'm wearing them for a reason," Billie said. She slowly walked in front of them, eyeing each one in turn.

"And that might be?" Roy asked, his voice trembling.

"Why?" Billie replied.

"Yes, why?" Roy muttered.

"Well, gents, I'm dressed this way because I am taking over my father's role in the lumber business," Billie said, not surprised when she heard gasps erupting among the men. "I plan to keep my father's dream alive. I learned enough about the business when he lived in Seattle. He taught me all the tricks of the trade, so to speak. I know all about felling trees, and anything else you might question me about. Nothing'll change under my leadership, gents. You'll get the same pay for the same duties you performed for my father."

She looked at Roy, then at the lumberjacks again. "Are you game?" she asked, placing her hands on her hips. "Do you mind having a female giving orders to you alongside Roy?"

"We're game," one of the men said, nodding. "It's just good to know that we'll not be out of jobs."

"Your jobs are secure as long as you do them well enough," Billie said, then stopped directly in front of Roy. "Well, partner, what do you think?"

"Partner?" Roy muttered, but didn't say anything else.

He saw this two ways. If she did this, perhaps she wouldn't discover that he was no longer part owner of the company. She seemed concerned only with continuing her pa's business.

But he did see it in another light, too.

Wouldn't he look like a fool, having to work alongside a woman who had the same power her father had had? No, he just couldn't accept this.

But he would have to take it slow and work out how to rid his life of her—just as he had her pa!

Chapter Four

As he dismounted from his steed and walked it to its corral, Proud Eagle glanced at his home, where his son, Many Winds, awaited him . . . and where no wife would greet him with a sweet embrace and kiss.

When visions of his wife came to him, he felt guilty for thinking the white woman was beautiful. He had always thought that his wife was the most beautiful woman in the world. An ache encircled his heart as he thought of how Soft Wing had died so needlessly. A mud slide had come upon his people during a fierce rain and swallowed up many of them as they worked inside their lodges.

Proud Eagle had been away from his longhouse with his son that day. They had been on a fishing outing and had just made it safely back to shore after getting caught in the downpour.

Too many trees had been felled by the white lumberjacks on the high hill that stood behind his village. When he had seen the mud sliding down, he had stood frozen to the spot, for he knew that he could not move fast enough to warn anyone. It had happened so quickly.

He had lost his parents and his wife in the mud slide, as well as so many beloved people of his White Owl Clan. In his heart he carried a vengeance that he had forced himself not to act upon, but he would never forget or forgive the men who felled those trees and left the land vulnerable to the rains.

The white woman he had seen at the lumber baron's mansion grieved over this man's death. Proud Eagle cheered it. But he knew that losing only one man would not stop the felling of trees close to his people's homes. It was up to Proud Eagle to make certain it never happened again.

He had rebuilt his house and helped to build others, making certain that this time they were strong enough to stand against anything. Although the homes were traditional Makah longhouses made of split cedar planks placed horizontally and lashed to upright poles with lengths of twisted cedar withes, he had seen to it that the rebuilt homes had twice as much support as usual. The nearly flat roofs rested on huge roof beams placed atop posts set into the ground.

Inside his own lodge were five rooms, one for storage of his fishing gear, another for his lumbering equipment, and a bedroom each, one for his son, and one for himself.

The large outer room sufficed for both relaxing and cooking. However, since his wife and mother had died, the women of the village had been supplying him and his son with their meals.

But he hoped one day to find another woman whom he could love and take into his home. She would cook, filling the air with the aromas of baked bread and steamed fish, and she would be a mother to his son.

In a flash, the face of the flame-haired woman came to him again. He could not help but think that she was a vision of loveliness. But she seemed to be kin to the aggressive lumber baron who had brought such anger and heartache to Proud Eagle's people.

Knowing that his son and food awaited him, Proud Eagle hurried inside his longhouse.

He found Many Winds laughing and wrestling with his dog, whose thick, curly fur was as white as the snow that inspired his name. They were near the fireplace, and from the flames lapping around them, Proud Eagle could tell that his son had recently placed fresh wood on the grate.

At the outer fringes of the fire, in the hot coals, sat three pots that gave off pleasant aromas. Proud Eagle recognized one of his favorites—roasted egg-size wappatoe roots, which were harvested by the women from a nearby marsh.

He also smelled skunk cabbage warming in a pot beside the fire, and salmon, made into patties and always delicious.

"Father!" Many Winds squealed as he saw him standing just inside the doorway. He flew into Proud

Eagle's arms and hugged him. "Where have you been for so long? Both my tummy and Snow's are growling."

"I know," Proud Eagle said, returning the hug. He walked with Many Winds into the room, and Snow followed them, wagging his tail. "My stomach has been growling, too. Let us sit and eat. Then I shall tell you where I have been. But first you tell me what you have been doing while I was gone."

"I played with Snow, nothing more," Many Winds said as Proud Eagle sat down with his son on the pelts spread before the fireplace.

Many Winds had brought wooden plates and mugs of a sweet drink.

"You love your dog a lot, do you not?" Proud Eagle said, reaching for one pot and then the others.

He looked at Many Winds fondly. The boy looked like a small replica of himself. His mother had told Proud Eagle more than once that even at age three, Many Winds was Proud Eagle all over again, in his features and in his stance.

His raven-black hair fell down past his waist, long and flowing. He wore buckskin breeches, shirt, and moccasins. And although only eight winters of age now, he already showed a muscled body.

"I do love Snow a lot," Many Winds said, stroking his pet's thick fur. His dog was from one of the litters bred by the Makah for their fleecy fur, which was used by the women for making blankets and warm coats for the long days and nights of winter. "But I shall miss him, Father, when I go to school."

"Yes, but you know that you cannot take him with you. It is a rule. Dogs are not allowed there," Proud Eagle said, as he put some of the salmon on a plate for Snow, then prepared platters of food for both himself and his son.

"But, Father, I am the son of a *chief*," Many Winds whined drawing Proud Eagle's eyes to him in quick disapproval.

"You *are* the son of a chief, so speak like one, not like someone who feels the world owes him more than anyone else," Proud Eagle scolded.

He handed Many Winds his plate of food. "Now eat," he said in a less stern voice. "We will not discuss taking Snow to school again. Do you understand?"

"Yes, I understand," Many Winds said, holding back a sob.

"Son, you know that you cannot be treated with favoritism," Proud Eagle further explained when he saw the sadness in his son's dark eyes. "Resentments will build among the other children, and even the adults, were I to allow you to take your dog when no other child can take theirs."

"Yes, I understand," Many Winds said once again. "And I am sorry for behaving badly. But . . . but . . . I do dread going to school. I will not like living away from you and Snow. Why must we children be forced to do that? Is it not bad enough that we are forced to go to a white man's school, being taught by white people?"

"It is for your own good that you learn their ways," Proud Eagle said solemnly. "If we are to live among whites and not allow them to outsmart us, an education is very important."

"But to have to live there?" Many Winds asked, his eyes wavering as he glanced at his father.

"Treaty requires this of the Makah children," Proud Eagle explained, as he had countless times before. "You must go to school the day after tomorrow, for you are the last to go this autumn. I was wrong to allow you to stay home longer than the others, even if for only two days. Had you not complained of a sore throat you would have gone when the other children did."

Proud Eagle stopped long enough to eat from his plate, yet he scarcely tasted the food. He did not want to think about his son being away from him for any amount of time. Many Winds was all the family that Proud Eagle had left. Nights without him would be so lonely, so empty.

But his attending school and living there was necessary. It was required.

Proud Eagle knew that an education benefited the Makah children. It would strengthen their ability to cope with whites. If he didn't think it was important, he would have fought the ruling handed down by the United States government.

"Father, you have not yet told me what you did today," Many Winds said, as he finished eating, then reached for his dog. Snow curled up on his lap and was asleep in a second.

"I was riding Midnight, looking things over," Proud Eagle said. "I wanted to check out the activity around the white lumber baron's property."

"And what did you see?" Many Winds asked, his dark eyes wide.

"Not much," Proud Eagle said, but he recalled the lovely woman he had seen. He wondered who she was.

"I took a short nap while you were gone," Many Winds said, his voice breaking. "I—I—dreamed about Mother. In the dream she was so sweet and gentle." He lowered his eyes. "I miss Mother so much."

Proud Eagle set his empty plate aside and reached for Many Winds' hand. "Son, I miss her, too," he said sadly. "But as I have taught you, life must go on. Each day, you make new memories for when you are an old man dreaming of his past."

"My memories are still too filled with Mother," Many Winds said. "I do not want to replace them."

"In time you will find it much easier," Proud Eagle said, now caught up in his own memories of Soft Wing.

It was still hard for Proud Eagle to believe that his wife was dead—and all because the white lumber baron had felled trees so carelessly. Since then Proud

Eagle had felt nothing but loathing for the man and those who worked under his leadership.

The mud had been cleared, the dead buried, and the longhouses rebuilt. But no matter how many homes had been rebuilt, the graves of those who had died caused a bitterness toward the white man in Proud Eagle's heart. He fought these feelings every day with every fiber of his being, for he knew that bitterness was only hurtful.

He thought of the new trees now sprouting on that ravaged land, trees that Proud Eagle and his warriors had planted purposely to avoid another devastating mud slide in the future.

"Father, why can't I just learn from you?" Many Winds asked, interrupting Proud Eagle's thoughts.

"My son, you have already learned a wealth of knowledge from your father and your grandfather," Proud Eagle answered. "Now you must build on that foundation. You will be better prepared for manhood. You will be better prepared to deal with whites who might try to steal from our people. Had the Makah been taught the white ways sooner, no land would have ever been taken from us. There would be no white lumberjacks now in competition with the Makah for the land and trees. There would have been no treaties written up by whites that affect the lives of our people."

"Then I shall go without any more questions about it," Many Winds said. He lowered his eyes for a moment, then looked willfully up at his father again.

"But only because it is your sincere wish that I should do so."

"My son," Proud Eagle said, resting a hand on Many Winds' shoulder. "The only thing that you and the other Makah children can learn is to be better people. And no matter how hard whites try to undermine our people's power, the family will remain at the heart of Makah society. Remember that.

"I am proud of you," Proud Eagle continued with a smile. "I always shall be."

Many Winds smiled up at his father, too, even while making plans that would greatly disappoint him.

Chapter Five

To prove that she could do anything the other lumberjacks could do—choosing, marking and cutting the trees—Billie was working alongside the men.

She was using a wooden wedge, hammered with a stone maul, to split a plank cleanly from a straight-grained cedar. She ignored the occasional looks that were a combination of feelings: some of resentment, others of admiration when a man would stop and stare at her in her shirt, breeches, and boots, her hair coiled beneath a wide-brimmed hat.

When she had said that she was not selling her father's business, they hadn't expected her to work alongside them. When she had arrived at the bunkhouse at daybreak, announcing that she would be joining them, she ignored the gasps of horror.

As a teenager, she had often dreamed of working with her father and his lumberjacks. Yet she knew that she never would. Instead she had become the socialite her mother had always wanted her to be.

She attended balls in fancy gowns and enjoyed the admiration of handsome young men.

But whenever she could, she had sneaked out of their mansion to be with her father. She was glad now that she had done that. Those moments were precious to her. And knowing how much he loved his lumber company spurred her to try to keep his dream alive by running it herself.

But she was realizing today just how hard it was going to be. She had been away from physical labor for far too long. Had she truly believed that she could switch from being a "lady" to being a "lumberjane" without any problem?

The longer she stayed in the forest working alongside the men, the more she realized that this was not at all what she wanted out of life. It wasn't that she wanted to return to the socialite world either. She just wanted something that was genuine and everlasting.

But from all of the men she had become acquainted with in Seattle, she had concluded that there were no men anywhere who would please her. And it wasn't because she compared everyone with her father, as so many daughters were wont to do. She just had not found the man with that perfect smile and the right combination of gentleness and strength.

So what would she do if she decided not to continue her father's company even though she'd told the lumberjacks that she was staying? Where would she go? She had sold everything she owned and had cut all ties in Seattle.

"And so where has your mind wandered to, Billie Boy?"

Roy's voice broke through her thoughts.

She turned to him and said, "You do your job, I'll do mine, and never mind what I was thinking about. Just you keep your mind on business. We don't want any accidents on the job."

"Like your pa, who got careless that day?" Roy said, walking away from Billie. He looked at her over his shoulder. "Billie Boy, you'd best watch yourself, or you might be added to that graveyard alongside your pa."

A cold chill raced down Billie's spine. She thought she heard a threat in Roy's tone.

When she thought hard and long about her father's death and how it could have happened after years of his being so careful, she could not help but wonder if the accident had not been an accident after all.

But she didn't have proof. And the men who had worked for her father seemed to be staunch friends with Roy. Anything they had seen that day when the tree crashed down on her father and killed him instantly was surely locked away.

She took a handkerchief from her pocket and mopped the sweat from her brow as she watched Roy walk away from her. The sun streaming down through the leaves onto his bald head made it look like a strange, shiny ball. She wanted to shout at him how she felt, to put him in his place once and for all, but she realized that the men working near her had stopped to stare at her. She thrust her handkerchief back in her pocket.

"Get back to work," she ordered. "We've more than one tree to fell today."

They grumbled and returned to their work, pounding the wooden wedge again with the stone maul. The towering cedar tree they were working on started to sway.

"It's about ready to fall!" one of the men shouted. "Just put a little more muscle behind it, fellas, and we've got us another beaut!"

But they stopped again when the sound of an approaching horse came to them on the wind.

Billie turned and quickly recognized the muscled black stallion and the man riding it. It was the same handsome warrior that she had seen yesterday.

She was not sure how to feel about his coming here today. Was it to cause trouble? Was it to make demands of her and the lumberjacks? She remembered the previous trouble between the Makah chief and her father.

Wanting to ignore the warrior, Billie glared at the men. "What are you waiting for? Continue working."

"But it could be dangerous," one of the men argued. "The chief. He's riding where the tree will fall."

"Chief?" Billie said, her heart skipping a beat. This was Chief Proud Eagle?

"That's Proud Eagle," one of the men confirmed. "Miss Shaughnessy, we'd best wait until he's gone. We don't want no trouble with the Injuns, not any more than we already have."

"What sort of trouble are you talking about?" Billie asked.

"There was a mud slide," Roy said, joining the conversation. "The chief accused us of causing it. We've had to be careful since. There are way more Injuns in this area than lumberjacks."

"A mud slide?" Billie said, getting all sorts of visions in her mind's eye about the problems a mud slide could cause. "Where was it? How did it happen?"

They didn't get the chance to answer her, for Chief Proud Eagle rode up and drew a tight rein.

Billie wasn't sure why her heart was beating so erratically. But it was. She knew that its fierce pounding wasn't from fear. It was something more.

"I have warned you about cutting this close to my people's homes," Proud Eagle said angrily. "You will pay if you do not heed my warning and move farther back."

Proud Eagle's eyes widened with shock when Billie turned around and took her hat off, her brilliant red hair tumbling across her shoulders and down her back. She looked defiantly back at him with a steady stare, then stepped closer to his horse, one hand on her hip.

It was hard for her to remain steadfast when she found herself being so closely scrutinized by perhaps the most handsome man in the world.

But she had always found that those men who were classified as "handsome" were too caught up in their looks to be anything but boring. Surely it was no different with this Indian chief. Perhaps he was even more arrogant. She recalled her father calling Proud Eagle charming.

As she was glaring at Proud Eagle, her thoughts about him scrambling, Proud Eagle stared back at her. This woman was the same one that he had seen yesterday, but today she was clothed much differently. Today she wore the clothes of a man. And it stunned him that she was working side by side with the men, felling trees.

Yes, it did seem mysterious to him, definitely intriguing. He would want to know her better.

"Get off my land." Billie finally found the courage to speak, fighting to keep strength in her voice.

She had never been weak in the knees before, yet at this moment her legs actually felt rubbery.

"Get off and stay off," she repeated, daring him this time with flashing eyes.

"Your land?" Proud Eagle said, raising an eyebrow. "Who gave it to you?"

"It's none of your business," Billie said, still fighting to keep her voice even and demanding.

"As I told the lumber baron who recently died, and this man named Roy, what you are doing is wrong," Proud Eagle said. "By treaty, you are cutting far too close to my people's land."

"I don't believe a treaty would say anything of the

kind," Billie said stiffly. "Either the land is free to cut on, or it's not. By treaty, this strip of land is no longer yours. It's mine. And because it is, I can do whatever I wish with it."

"You keep saying it is yours," Proud Eagle said, leaning forward to gaze more intently into her wide green eyes. "Again I ask what makes it yours?"

"And again I say it is none of your business," Billie replied.

"It is my business," Proud Eagle said in a tight voice. "These trees and what you are doing with them is my business. My people take only what we need. You take any and all. And you are cutting wrong. You should be leaving enough trunk to sustain new growth."

"And so now you are trying to tell me how to cut trees?" Billie said, finding this man incredibly stubborn.

"I only say what is true," Proud Eagle said in a softer voice. "If you would listen and do as I suggest, you would, in the end, have more trees, not less."

"Billie, move aside. I'll take care of this," Roy said, suddenly stepping between Billie and Proud Eagle. "I've heard all of this before. Chief, you're wasting your breath. Go home, Proud Eagle. Leave us be. We've more work to do before it gets dark."

Billie glared at Roy's back, then stepped around in front of him and stared into his pale gray eyes. "Who told you to interfere?" she said, her voice filled with venom. "I'm capable of taking care of this."

"Billie, how dare you talk to me like that in front of the men and this Injun chief?" Roy growled. "Must I remind you that I . . ."

"I need no reminders of who or what you are," Billie said, her eyes snapping.

She leaned closer to him. "You might think that you are my partner, but let me tell you one thing, Roy Clawson," she said in a low hiss so Proud Eagle couldn't hear her words. "My father put up with you. I don't have to."

"But Billie—" Roy started.

"No buts, Roy," Billie cut him off, her voice still quiet and low. "I have my own idea about how Father died. If I ever discover that you had a role in it, by damn, Roy, I'll shoot you."

Roy glared at her for a moment longer, then turned on his heel and walked far away from the men. In his heart he felt such hate, such contempt, that he knew he would have to do something about Billie Boy very soon.

As Billie turned to order Proud Eagle off the land again, he gave her a steady stare, then wheeled his horse around and rode off.

Hardly able to think straight, Billie could only watch him go.

"Billie Boy is intrigued by an Injun," Roy said as he sidled up close to her. "Billie Boy cain't take her eyes off the handsome chief!"

Anger shot through Billie and she slapped Roy hard across his face, then turned to the men. "Come on!" she ordered, ignoring the angry fire that leaped into Roy's eyes. "We've got more work here."

Feeling much more comfortable without the hat, she dropped it on the ground and resumed working on the tree until it finally fell.

Billie then stood back from the men and again mopped her brow with her handkerchief.

"One more tree and then we will go," she said, still unnerved by the encounter with Proud Eagle.

She forced thoughts of him out of her mind and went to the next tree that her father had marked to be cut. Roy had pointed out where her father had died, only a short distance from where this tree stood.

Her heart ached when she saw the ground there.

She glared at Roy. She got such a feeling of foreboding when she considered that Roy might have had a role in her father's death.

She had to find out the truth.

If Roy was indeed behind her father's death, he would rue the day he had ever lifted a hand against her family. She would see that he paid.

"In one way or another," she whispered to herself.

Chapter Six

Billie arrived at her bedroom bedraggled and worn out. She stood before a full-length mirror and stared at herself. She was still angry over her unexpected meeting with Proud Eagle.

He had disarmed her with his handsomeness, his muscles, his midnight-black eyes and his long, thick hair. Strange how even now she wished that she could run her fingers through that hair.

"What am I doing?" she whispered. She reached up to touch her own hair. It was wet and frizzy with sweat, and its stench made her nostrils flare.

Billie grabbed a pair of scissors and began cutting her long hair, one lock at a time. She rationalized that with short hair she would be more comfortable while working alongside the lumberjacks. She would even look more like a man.

When she finished, she realized exactly what she had done. In the mirror she saw how short she had cut her hair, leaving only tight ringlets. Suddenly tears came to her eyes.

"I look horrid!" she cried. "He will see me as ugly."

She was stunned to find herself worrying about what Proud Eagle would think. He had been her father's enemy. And now he was hers.

"*My* enemy," she whispered aloud in an effort to convince herself.

Earlier she had decided that this life of felling trees was not what she wanted to do. But now, she had stepped into a trap of her own making. Her anger at Roy and the Makah chief fueled Billie's desire to test her mettle. Yet if she proved it, did that mean she would have to stay with lumbering?

"Father, what am I to do?" she whispered as she closed her eyes and saw him in her mind's eye. "What would you have me do?"

Chapter Seven

Proud Eagle was in his longhouse sitting before the fire. He could not get the flame-haired woman out of his mind.

He was certainly surprised by how she was dressed, and even more by how she had sided with the lumberjacks. He was stunned by her open antagonism toward him when she didn't even know him personally. Not only was she working with the men, but she was looking like them too. How could a beautiful woman want to look like a man?

And she, not Roy Clawson, seemed to be in charge of the lumberjacks. The way she had spoken to Roy, putting him in his place and clearly showing animosity toward him, had proved she didn't care for him.

Surely she was kin to the dead lumber baron.

He forced himself to stop thinking about her and the white men. His son needed him now. Tomorrow Many Winds would be leaving home to stay at the

school. Proud Eagle already felt the loneliness that
his son's absence would bring him.

He looked over his shoulder at Many Winds, who
had fallen asleep on his pallet beside the fire with
Snow in his arms.

Proud Eagle went to his son and ran a hand
through his thick black hair. "My son, I want only
what is best for you," he whispered. "Today I again
discovered just how determined whites can be. They
sent a woman to do a man's job!"

"How do you feel about Billie Boy now?" Roy
stood before the men in the bunkhouse, his fists on
his hips.

They frowned at him, then one spoke for them all.

"We don't like her and her bossiness one bit," he
grumbled. "No woman should be ordering men
around. What are you going to do about it, Roy?"

He kneaded his chin as he gazed up at the ceiling.
"I see her as weak even though she pretends to be
strong," he said. "I think the Injun already has some
sort of hold on her. I saw it in her eyes as she looked
at the man. Although she tried to look strong and
determined, there was something about her voice
that proved otherwise. We've got to put a stop to
that, now."

He pulled his flask out of his pocket, took a swallow of whiskey, then handed it to one of the men.
"Take a swig, then pass it on," he said. "What we've
got to remember here is that Billie is a woman. I'll

come up with a plan to put her in her rightful place. Are you all game?"

He saw that some in the group seemed to suddenly shy away, and he realized that in time, he would need to weed out the weak.

Chapter Eight

After a restless night, Billie had risen early to take a ride on the horse that had been her father's favorite, a strawberry roan.

She did not know exactly where she was going, but she felt a ride would clear her mind. She had to find a way to proceed with this new life that had been handed to her.

The sun had risen some time ago from behind the tall, lovely Norway pines and now shone in a turquoise sky. Billie made a right turn and rode up a slight incline that looked out over the ocean.

She glimpsed several American bald eagles soaring over the water and realized how the Makah town of Eagle Bay had gotten its name. It was wonderful to see, so peaceful, so serene . . . so beautiful!

Farther out at sea, a lone whale surfaced then dove deeply into the water.

She rode onward, enjoying being one with nature instead of being with the sweating, foulmouthed lumberjacks.

She could see why her father had come to this land. There was so much beauty to behold.

Behind her, in the forests, was a wealth of plant and wildlife, nature in all its glory. She could hear the birdcalls echoing from tree to tree. She could smell the fragrance of autumn flowers that grew along the forest floor.

Her adventure had led her to a hilltop that overlooked the Makah village.

It occurred to her what had kept her awake through her long, sleepless night. She had not wanted to admit it to herself, but the reason was Proud Eagle. No matter how hard she had tried, she had not been able to get him off her mind.

She had vowed to herself not to allow him to enchant her, yet there she was, totally taken with the Makah chief. And now she was close to his village, spying on his people, hoping to get a glimpse of him.

Thus far she had not seen him, but she was intrigued enough by what she saw to linger a while longer.

The Makah homes were longhouses made of cedar and arranged in rows close to the beach. They were grouped together along the shoreline, yet far enough back so that high tide could not reach them. What looked like halibut waved like white flags on the longhouse flat roofs, on drying racks.

The village was a sea settlement, vibrating with human existence.

She watched as women took shellfish from the rocky shoreline and placed them in wicker baskets.

Young children, boys and girls alike, no older than five or six years of age, did their part by keeping watch over the piles of fresh fish that had been brought to shore by the men. The children chased away bothersome crows and the occasional seagull that would suddenly swoop down from the sky for a fast, easy meal of fish.

Back in Seattle, Billie had taken the time to study and learn what she could about the Makah tribe.

They seemed to center their lives around lumbering, yet did some fishing for themselves, and for trading. In her studies she had learned what fish they caught and how.

She watched now as herring were being caught on the bone points of rakes that the men were sweeping through the shallow water. Down the shore, smelt were being taken in fine-mesh dip nets.

The nets had been of particular interest to her, as she had discovered that they took a great deal of time and energy to make and required careful drying and storing to prevent rot.

She knew, too, that lingcod and bass preferred rocky places. The lingcod could be lured to the surface from the shallow bottoms where they spawned and took up guard to protect their eggs. They were speared at the surface.

Halibut were caught out at sea, and the Makah

were known to bring in quite a large harvest of them when they needed to restock their store of fish.

She watched the interesting scene of gathering the fish, then saw some women coming into the village with heaping baskets of bright red wild strawberries. Their children followed closely behind, their mouths and hands red from eating the luscious fruit that they had helped to pick.

She gazed again at the village as a whole and saw a calm, peaceful atmosphere where everyone seemed loving and happy.

After observing this scene, Billie could not help but feel guilty about what her father and the United States government had done to the Makah. She realized that her father might have been up to no good as far as the Makah were concerned. Had he ignored the treaties? And worse, had he duped the Makah?

If he had used underhanded tactics against these people, she would rather not carry on what he had started.

She wished now that she was back in Seattle, continuing her mother's millinery shop, instead of trying to run a lumber company. She had been in Eagle Bay only a few days, and already she had discovered that she hated this sort of life.

She hated the lumber business. It was not at all as she remembered it as a young girl. Yesterday, she had wanted to feel the same way she had when she had been with her father in the forest, felling trees outside of Seattle. She had wanted to enjoy being in charge of the lumberjacks, as her father had been when he was alive.

But she just didn't want this life.

Yet for her father, should she ignore her own desires and keep his dream alive? Is that what he would have wanted for her?

She had an important decision to make now that she was in charge of her own life.

And she had Roy Clawson to worry about. She certainly didn't want to hand her father's business over to him.

Pushing her thoughts aside, she continued watching the Makah people. Suddenly, she realized that the only children she saw were very young, the oldest perhaps five or six. She wondered where the older children were.

Afraid that someone might see her there, Billie yanked her reins and wheeled her horse around. She rode down from the hill, then on along a straight stretch of ground away from the village.

Reaching up to her hair, she groaned when she was reminded of what she had done. Although cutting her hair had been part of her plan, she wished now that she had not been so foolish.

The more she thought about how Proud Eagle had looked at her dressed in men's clothes—a look of utter surprise and something else that she could not define—the more embarrassed she felt.

Although she told herself it should not matter to her how he felt, deep down, where her desires as a woman were formed, it did. For the first time in her life she truly cared what a man thought of her.

She had spent time with many men, attending balls, the opera, the symphony. But they had meant nothing more to her than an escort.

Her mother had wanted her to marry a wealthy man. She wanted her to live in a mansion that overlooked Puget Sound and attend all of the fancy functions that Seattle offered. But her mother's dream had not come to fruition. She had died before Billie found the right man.

Now she rode onward for some time, then slowed when she saw a two-storied white house in the distance. She didn't know of any people living in this area, so she could only wonder whose house this was.

Young children, boys and girls alike, were playing inside a white picket fence. She was too curious not to investigate.

When she got closer to the house, she realized that the children were all copper-skinned—Makah. There were many, ranging in age from eight years to perhaps fifteen. They seemed happy enough as they ran around playing a game of tag and laughing.

She thought back to the small children that she had seen at the Makah village and assumed that these children were also from there.

But why? What were they doing away from their people?

Finally just outside of the fence, Billie dismounted.

As she flung her reins around a hitching rail, she saw that the children had stopped playing. They had grown quiet as they stared at her, some clinging to each other.

Billie smiled at them, but they didn't return the smile.

Her eyes were then drawn to a sign just above the porch door: RAINBOW BOARDINGHOUSE.

Billie found it hard to connect a boardinghouse with children. Why would they be there instead of with their families?

Suddenly a heavyset, fat-jowled white woman, her hair coiled into a tight gray bun atop her head, came out onto the porch. She clapped her hands loudly and told the children that playtime was over.

They hurried into the house.

The woman now focused her attention on Billie, and she came toward her.

Realizing that she looked conspicuous standing there staring, Billie met the woman halfway and extended her hand in friendship.

"I am Billie Shaughnessy," she said.

"My name is Anna Thompson," the woman replied, gripping Billie's hand tightly. "Why are you here? What do you want?"

Billie could see the woman studying her questioningly. "I'm new in the area," she answered. "I was just out for a ride on my horse and saw the children."

She allowed her eyes to drift to the sign above the door, then back to Anna.

"I am headmistress of this boardinghouse," Anna said. "Would you like to come in and see how dutiful the Makah children are and how eager they are to learn?"

Billie's eyes widened. "You just called this a boardinghouse, yet you speak of a classroom. I don't understand."

"Some refer to it as a boardinghouse, some as a boarding school," Anna said. "In truth, it is a school, but the children live here year-round until they are older. If a child is very good, as a treat, he or she is occasionally allowed to go home on a weekend. Sometimes a family member brings a picnic lunch that they share with their child outside the classroom."

Billie was shocked. She wondered who had set up such rules and why the Makah people agreed to them. All that she had read about Indians showed their complete dislike of compromising with whites about anything.

She would think that allowing their children to be taken away to a boardinghouse school would be one of the worst things that could happen to them.

"Come inside and see how things are set up," Anna said, gesturing toward the building. "I'm quite proud of how things work here."

"Yes, I would like to see," Billie said, quite curious.

She followed Anna into the house and then into a large room, where children of all ages sat on seats behind desks.

The children were doing mathematics as a slight teacher with golden hair wrote numbers on a blackboard with a piece of white chalk.

Billie looked from child to child. There were both boys and girls. Some of the boys had a defiant look in their eyes, while others had a strange eagerness. The girls sat straight, poised and polite. Many wore a veil of non-expression, not revealing how they felt about what they were being made to do. Others had expressions that were hard for Billie to read.

"The teacher's name is Freda," Anna said. "She is quite good at what she does. The children adore her.

"Come with me," Anna urged then, nodding toward the door.

She took Billie to her private office, where golden sunlight poured in through the several windows. A desk sat at one end, and comfortable-looking chairs sat at the other before a fireplace.

"Sit down and have coffee with me," Anna said, nodding toward the chairs.

"Thank you," Billie said.

After Billie got settled in a chair and had accepted a cup of coffee, Anna sat down beside her, also with coffee in hand.

"This school has been the best thing that could have happened to the Makah," Anna declared. She took a sip of coffee, then set the cup on a table beside her. "This boarding school was established solely for the Indian children. The intent was to remove the children from the influence of the elders of their tribes, who teach them ways of the past. Here the children are instructed that the traditional ways of their people are evil and backward. Only by these means, it is felt, can the young people attain the values and scholarly accomplishments necessary for assimilation into the white society."

Billie was stunned. As the woman continued talking about the school and about how the children had to adapt to the rules of the whites, Billie could not help but recall the crude adage "Kill the Indian but save the man"—an apt summary of the school's philosophy.

She was appalled by it.

"I am surprised that the Makah have allowed their children to be sent away to school," Billie said hesitantly. "The boys are surely needed to help with the fishing, and the girls are needed by their mothers."

Billie remembered the children helping at the village now and realized why she had seen only small ones there. The others were being forced to attend this school.

"The boarding school was established by treaty for the sake of the Makah children," Anna said. "Yes, they *are* needed at their villages, but the children are gone from their homes for only a few years. They come at age eight and return home again at age fifteen. By that time the girls have become ladies and the boys have become men, an age when they would normally be most helpful to their parents anyway."

"I see," Billie said quietly, trying to be kind to the overbearing and unlikable woman.

"The first agents assigned to this land had difficulty in persuading the Makah parents to send their children to the boarding school, even though it is the law," Anna said severely. "I was told that by jailing one father and threatening similar punishment to others, the first agents were able to gain a quota of students."

"I see—a quota," Billie said. She needed to escape quickly, for she could not tolerate this much longer.

"The parents are allowed to visit their children in the large sitting room," Anna said, then broke off sharply as she heard footsteps approaching and then stopping at her door.

"Why, Chief Proud Eagle," Anna said, beaming as she hurried to him. "And, ah, Many Winds. I am so glad you finally brought your son to our school."

Billie felt the heat of a blush as her eyes met and held Proud Eagle's.

His gaze slid to her hair, and Billie saw his expression change quickly to something akin to horror.

Yes, she knew how she looked with her hair cut off, and she hated it even more at this moment.

She had met Proud Eagle only briefly, but now, after seeing him a third time, she knew that she felt something special for a man for the very first time in her life. It was regrettable that he was an Indian.

"Please excuse me," Anna said over her shoulder to Billie. "I must tend to business."

Billie watched Anna whisk Proud Eagle and the child beside him away. For a moment she could not move. She hadn't expected to see Proud Eagle again so soon. She thought that the next time they would meet would be during another confrontation among the trees.

She raised her hand to her hair and ran her fingers through the short red locks. "Oh, why did I do something so rash?" she whispered, cringing as she remembered taking the scissors to her hair. Sighing, she left the room, and then the house.

She hurried to her horse, noticing the black stallion hitched next to her roan. She knew he belonged to Proud Eagle. Just seeing the beautiful animal sent a sensual shiver racing across her flesh and a blush rushing to her cheeks.

"I must stop thinking about him," she told herself firmly.

She grabbed her reins, mounted the horse, and rode away from the school at a gallop, forcing herself not to look back.

Chapter Nine

"Many Winds, this is Anna Thompson, the headmistress of the school," Proud Eagle said as his son gave the dowdy, plump woman a stubborn stare. "She will take you to the classroom where the other children are and will introduce you to the teacher."

"Father, I do not want to go," Many Winds said, his voice breaking.

Anna took Many Winds' hand. "Come, child. Your friends have already become acquainted with the teacher. Now so shall you. After the class is over for the day and you children have been fed, you will be shown to your bed."

"I have placed his bag of clothes just inside the front door," Proud Eagle said, sadness tugging at his heart at leaving his son there.

But he knew it was for the best, so he walked out without looking at Many Winds again.

Once he was outside, Proud Eagle saw Billie riding away in the distance.

He wanted to ask Anna Thompson why the white woman was there. Surely she was snooping. But he would never ask, for he did not want anyone to guess his feelings for the beautiful woman.

He was angry at himself for being attracted to her. She was his rival and his enemy.

His thoughts still on the woman, he grabbed his reins and mounted his steed. He wondered what had happened to her hair. Why would a woman cut such beautiful hair?

Had she done this to make herself blend in better with the men as she worked alongside them? Or had she done it out of mourning for the death of the lumber baron?

No matter why, though, he could not help but feel regret over the deed. He had enjoyed looking at her long red hair.

Knowing that he should be thinking not about her at all but about the son he had just left with whites, Proud Eagle took one last look at the boarding school before riding away. He felt an emptiness in his heart, but he knew that he had had no choice.

He believed that it was for the good of the Makah children that they were there, learning. It would help them know how to fight the white man's laws when they grew into adults. It was hard, though.

He kept telling himself over and over again, that no matter how hard whites tried to undermine its power, family would always remain at the heart of Makah society. Yet, by going to school, his son and his brethren would learn how to best the white people in all things!

Chapter Ten

Night had just fallen, and the fire in his fireplace was cozy and warm. Proud Eagle sat before it trying to concentrate on anything but the woman, but to no avail. She was there in his mind's eye.

Suddenly something pushed her image aside.

"Snow," Proud Eagle whispered as he looked over his shoulder at the door, which he had left ajar for Snow's return.

It was not like Snow to stay outside after dark for very long. He was not as brave as Proud Eagle had hoped he would be. He had wanted to depend on Snow to protect Many Winds if they came upon danger in the forest together. But Proud Eagle doubted that would ever happen since Snow always crept away from danger with his tail tucked between his legs.

Just as he rose to go outside and whistle for the dog, he heard footsteps at his door.

Thinking it might be a warrior come to keep Proud Eagle company on his first night alone, he hurried to the door.

Even before he got to it, though, he could see through the partially open door that it was not a warrior friend.

"Anna Thompson?" he said, raising an eyebrow and opening the door farther.

The headmistress of the boarding school stood there, face full of concern and wariness. As Anna peered up at him, icy fingers of dread crept up and down his spine.

"Why have you come?" Proud Eagle asked. He gestured for her to come inside his lodge and stepped aside to allow it.

Anna started wringing her hands as she moved past him, then turned to face him again. "I have something to tell you that you won't be pleased with," she said, her voice audibly breaking.

Proud Eagle's heart skipped a beat.

"What has happened?" Proud Eagle asked, his voice tight. "What is it you are finding so hard to say to this Makah chief?"

"Many Winds has disappeared," Anna blurted out. "He . . . he . . . wasn't in his bed when I made my rounds to see that the children were tucked in. When I got to Many Winds' cot, he was not there."

"My son was left in your care, and you have let this happen?" Proud Eagle said, struggling to control his anger. He had depended on this woman and the teacher to keep his son safe.

"I apologize deeply," Anna said, her hands clasped behind her now, her courage returning.

"Many Winds must have truly hated being at the school, although I have always tried my best to make the children feel comfortable."

She lowered her eyes, then gazed up at Proud Eagle again, her voice hardened. "You know, Chief Proud Eagle, that even though he has shown such a dislike for the school, or perhaps for me or his teacher, he must still attend. I trust that after you find him, you will explain this to him. A child must know his place, even if he is the child of a Makah chief. And this child, along with the others, must attend my boarding school until they are of the age when they are no longer required to be there."

"When I find Many Winds, I will explain things to him again. He will return to the boarding school, not because of your threats, but because I know that it is necessary for the future of my child and all Makah children to learn what white children learn," Proud Eagle said stiffly. "Now, if you will excuse me, I must search for my son."

"I did not mean to sound as though I was threatening you," Anna said tersely. "I was just trying to explain things. That's all."

"Yes, I imagine that is what you meant to do, but nevertheless, the threat was there in your voice," Proud Eagle said. He stepped closer to her and spoke very clearly. "When my son returns to your boarding school, you will not use the tone of voice with him that you just used with me. If you do, I shall report you to those who have given you authority over the

Makah children. I will see that you are replaced. I hope you understand what I am saying."

"And now who is doing the threatening?" Anna said, her eyes flashing. With that, she swept past Proud Eagle.

He watched her stomp to the edge of the village, then board a horse and carriage. He was glad when she was gone, for her sort tainted the very earth upon which they walked. And his people's land was theirs and sacred in their eyes.

Proud Eagle left his longhouse and went from home to home until he had rounded up a good number of his warriors. They now stood beneath the bright moon's glow. Night had fallen with its dark shroud of black across Makah land as Proud Eagle told them what had happened.

"My son is missing," he repeated, his voice drawn. "I knew that he did not want to attend the boarding school, but I had no idea that he was this determined not to be there."

"We will find him for you," a warrior said.

"My son's dog, Snow, is also missing," Proud Eagle added. "Perhaps Many Winds came and got him. Earlier he had asked to take Snow with him, but I explained why it was forbidden to do so. If he left the school to get Snow, then it is obvious that he did not understand this rule."

"There are so many rules for our children that were set down by white man's law," another warrior said, his voice filled with anger and resentment. "Perhaps a day will come when our children will not be at the mercy of whites. We should build our own school!"

"It is in my heart, too, that this will be possible someday," Proud Eagle said. "But at this moment, we must concentrate on one thing—finding my son."

Suddenly he had a thought that made his heart go cold. Perhaps he was putting the blame for his son's absence on the wrong person. What if Roy Clawson and the white lumberjacks had something to do with Many Winds' disappearance? Might Roy have abducted him to use as ransom in order to get promises from Proud Eagle that he normally would not make about the land? Was this a way for Proud Eagle to be forced to give up more of his land to the white lumberjacks?

The lumber baron had used many sordid tactics in order to cheat the Makah. But Proud Eagle was clever about such things in his own right. The rich white man's ambitions to gain more land had not been realized before he died.

And the woman? What control did she have over the lumberjacks and the company? She had seemed to be in charge when Proud Eagle found her working alongside the lumberjacks in the forest. Next to her, Roy Clawson had seemed to be only second in command.

Proud Eagle could not envision the woman kidnapping a child for her own gain. When he had seen her at the school, she seemed interested in the children, but not in a devious way.

No, she could not have had anything to do with this, and he hoped that the lumberjacks had not either. He hoped that it was all Many Winds' doing. If so, he would be easily enough found and dealt with.

"Let us go now and search," Proud Eagle said.

His warriors nodded and soon they were all mounted and ready. They separated and went in different directions, with instructions to meet back at the village at dawn. If his son was not found by then, Proud Eagle would ponder the options that he faced.

His heart heavy, each mile he traveled without success caused more fear to build inside his chest. The fact that Snow was missing as well, made him suspect that Many Winds and his dog were together somewhere, perhaps lost.

Yes, surely that was what had happened. Many Winds had gotten lost in the dark, and when dawn came he would find his way back home.

Proud Eagle was determined to hold that hope within his heart. Distraught and weary, he watched dawn break along the horizon in beautiful streaks of magenta as the sun slowly crept up over the ocean. He sighed heavily and wheeled his horse around. He headed back toward their village, eager to rejoin the other warriors who also had ridden through the night. Proud Eagle hoped that others might have found Many Winds and be waiting for Proud Eagle's return.

The village came into view, and the glorious morning light glowed on the longhouses, but he saw no activity. He realized that he was returning to an emptiness that he had not felt since the deaths of his beloved mother, father, and wife. He felt the same despair now that losing his family had brought into his heart then. He now believed that his son might have met with a bad end out there somewhere in the dark.

He would not allow himself to think farther than that. Anger seethed within him as he thought of what evils the white men could do to an innocent Makah child.

But he must wait a while longer. He must not do anything rash, for he had to think of his people. They depended on him as their leader.

He rode on into the village and took his horse to his corral, then went to the council house to sit with the warriors who were already back and to await the return of the others. When at last they were all there and no one had brought good news of finding Many Winds, Proud Eagle hung his head and began softly chanting.

The others joined him until there was a great hum in the air. The sound brought the women and small children into the council house, and soon everyone was mourning the loss of someone beloved to them all.

Chapter Eleven

The sun was just barely visible along the horizon when Billie rode away from the stable. She had gotten up earlier than usual, dressed quickly in her riding skirt, knee-high leather boots, white blouse and leather jacket, and hurried out to the stable without anyone seeing her. She didn't want the lumberjacks, especially Roy, to know what she was doing.

She hadn't been able to get that odd look that Proud Eagle always gave her off her mind. She decided to go exploring again. But this time she wanted to see if she could discover exactly why the Makah hated her father—and now her—so much.

She had a map in her saddlebag. After studying it this morning, she knew exactly what land was supposed to be hers and what belonged to the Makah, by treaty.

As she traveled onward, riding farther and farther from the safety of her home, she became more ill by the moment, for she discovered that her father and Roy had gone far beyond the boundaries set by treaty. They had stripped land too close to the Makah village. And she could see that a mud slide was possible if it rained heavily.

She dismounted and studied the stumps of several of the trees. As knowledgeable as she was about felling trees, she knew that these had been cut only recently. Perhaps the Makah didn't even know about them yet.

"I must make certain that no more trees are cut on this stretch of land," she whispered to herself. She mounted and turned the strawberry roan toward home.

She must see that these boundaries were made right. She would go to Chief Proud Eagle and apologize for her father's bad behavior. His and Roy's schemes had gone against all that was right.

She could most certainly understand Proud Eagle's antagonism toward her. She was her father's daughter and had taken up the responsibilities that had once been his. She felt ashamed for having spoken so rudely to Proud Eagle herself. He must think she was as big a swindler as her father and Roy Clawson.

On her right, she saw the Indian village along the rocky shore at Eagle Bay. Her jaw tightened as she headed toward it.

She would not wait until later to apologize and tell Proud Eagle what she planned to do to right the injustice done against his people. She would tell him now.

Things would soon be different. The behavior

toward his people would be different. They would be treated fairly.

If Roy Clawson got in the way, then she would go to the authorities and would turn him in.

She felt sad over her father's role in the deception of the Makah and wished that she had been proven wrong about him. What she had discovered since her arrival clouded her good memory of him. As a child, she had idolized that tall, handsome man who seemed to know everything. She had secretly hoped to one day be as strong and as powerful as he.

But her mother had urged her to take a different road in life, one that Billie had ended up enjoying. She loved a fancy hat just as much as any other lady who frequented her mother's millinery shop.

Her thoughts were disturbed when she heard something akin to a soft whimper on her left. She had just entered a thick stand of aspen trees, with only enough room for her on her horse.

Some of their leaves had already turned golden, and as the wind whispered through them, they made a sound like softly falling rain.

But there again she heard the other sound. It sounded like someone was afraid . . . or in pain. She drew to a stop and looked carefully around.

A third time she heard it.

This time she could tell that it was a child crying.

She dismounted and tied her reins to a low limb, then moved stealthily toward the sound, which seemed to be coming from just inside a small cave.

"Who is there?" she finally shouted. "Why are you crying? Let me see you."

"I cannot step out," the tiny voice said between sobs. "I . . . I . . . am injured. A . . . a . . . spider crawled into my moccasin and bit my foot. It hurts too much for me to walk. Please help me."

Billie hurried toward the voice. "I'm coming," she reassured the child. "I'll help you."

At the cave, sun was flooding into the entrance, settling on a child, who sat gazing up at her. A dog was curled on his lap, trembling, its large eyes watching Billie.

She could tell that the dog was more afraid of her than the child was.

"It's you," she gasped when she saw that it was Proud Eagle's son. He was shivering and pale.

She could see by the path of tears through the dirt on his face that he had been crying for quite a while.

"Yes, it is I, Many Winds," he said. "I remember you. I saw you one day as I spied on the tall mansion. You were beside a grave."

"My father's," Billie said softly.

"Your father was the dead lumber baron?" Many Winds said, his eyes widening.

"Yes, he was my father," Billie said.

Many Winds swallowed hard. "I'm sorry he was your father," he said.

Billie was taken aback by his serious tone. "Why?"

"A man like him should be no one's father," Many Winds said solemnly.

Before Billie could respond, he blurted out, "I also saw you at the school."

"Yes, I saw you, too," Billie said.

"Please take me to my father," Many Winds said, suddenly sobbing. "I was bad. I . . . I . . . ran away from school."

Trying not to think about what Many Winds had said about her father, Billie knelt before him, and patted his cheek. The dog allowed her to do so but she realized that it seemed too afraid to move.

She gazed at the moccasin that lay beside the child, and then at his foot, which was red and swollen to almost twice its normal size.

"I'll get you home as quickly as I can," she told him, noting the feverish foot and glassy-eyed child. It was imperative to get him to his home and see that he was properly treated.

"Will your dog follow us if I put you on my horse to take you home?" Billie asked gently.

"I was so wrong," Many Winds sobbed. "But I wanted to be with my dog. I wasn't allowed to take him with me to school. I . . . I . . . missed him so much."

"Will he follow us?" Billie asked again.

"Yes, he will follow," Many Winds said. He lifted Snow so that their eyes met. "Did you hear, Snow? You must follow."

Billie picked up the lone moccasin that lay beside Many Winds and thrust it into a front pocket of her jacket while the boy eased Snow down onto the rocky floor of the cave. Billie swept the child into her arms, then hurried to her horse, the white, fleecy-coated dog following them.

"It hurts," Many Winds sobbed, cringing as pain shot through his foot. He clung to Billie. "My father is going to be mad at me. So is my teacher. And especially—"

Billie interrupted him. "No one is going to be mad," she assured him as she gently placed him on the horse. "Everyone will be too happy to see you to be mad. I'm certain they have been worried about you."

"I . . . I . . . am so sleepy now," Many Winds said, his voice getting weaker by the minute.

Billie mounted her horse and held her arm around Many Winds, who clung to her, his cheek resting on her chest.

"Go to sleep. I will get you home as quickly as I can," Billie murmured, urging her horse into a gallop. She looked over her shoulder and saw that Snow was dutifully following.

When she arrived at the village, small knots of people began to follow alongside her horse, trying to get a glimpse of Many Winds.

She was uneasy by their worried expressions and angry eyes as they looked from the child to her.

"Many Winds, you are home," Billie murmured. "You can wake up now."

She drew the horse to a stop, her insides clenching as she saw Proud Eagle exit a large longhouse. He stopped only for a second to make eye contact with Billie, before hurrying toward her.

"Father." Many Winds awakened, and tears

streamed from his eyes as Proud Eagle took him from Billie's arms.

Proud Eagle gave Billie a questioning look, then his eyes narrowed angrily. He could not help but think the worst.

But this was not the time for questions and anger. His son had been injured. He devoured Many Winds with his eyes, his gaze stopping on the swollen foot.

"He was awake when I found him in a cave," Billie said, dismounting. "He ran away from the school to get his dog, then went and hid in a cave. He said he was bit by a spider and it hurt too much to walk. I . . . I . . . hope the spider wasn't a poisonous one."

Proud Eagle could tell that the white woman was sincere in her concern for Many Winds. She had brought his son safely home. He owed her a debt that he would have to repay later.

For now, his son's well-being took precedence. He needed to be seen by Blue Cloud, his people's elderly shaman.

"I searched for my son but couldn't find him," Proud Eagle said, feeling guilty for having misjudged Billie. He held his son carefully and gazed down at his silent face.

"He was probably asleep when you went past the cave," Billie murmured.

"I know about the cave," Proud Eagle said, "but I didn't think to look there. He's afraid of the bats that live in the cave."

"I didn't see any," Billie said, then remembered the dog. "I imagine the dog kept them from the child."

"I must hurry him to my shaman," Proud Eagle said, unable to tear his gaze away from his son.

Billie followed Proud Eagle to Blue Cloud's lodge. She couldn't leave until she knew that the child was going to be all right.

She stood back and watched as the older man applied a poultice made from the inside bark of a skunk cabbage plant. As he began preparing another ointment, Billie knew it was time to leave.

The child would surely be all right now that he was being seen to by the man the Makah trusted, and this was not the time to admit to any wrongdoings that her father and Roy had perpetrated. Billie hurried to her horse.

As she grasped her reins, she saw Proud Eagle standing outside the shaman's house and looking in her direction. She understood why he didn't thank her. She understood too well the antagonism he must still feel toward her for all the evil brought upon his people by her father and Roy Clawson.

A time would come soon when they could talk, and when they did, she would explain what she was planning to do for him and his people.

"He has waited forever for his people to be treated right by whites, so I can wait just a little longer," she whispered to herself as she rode out of the village.

Chapter Twelve

By the next morning, Billie had made a decision. She was not going to work today, nor were the men. For now, the business was closed until she said otherwise. If Roy tried to take control and order his men to cut more trees, she would fire them all on the spot. She was her father's daughter, and she carried the power that came with that.

Determined to see that things went her way, Billie rode up to the bunkhouse, secured her horse's reins on the hitching rail, then stomped onto the porch and inside without knocking first.

The startled men looked up from their breakfast, as the cook stood over them, ladling out thick gravy over freshly made hot biscuits.

Billie stared back at them in stony silence, her eyes searching out Roy. He shared breakfast with the men every morning before heading out to the day's work site.

She didn't have to search far. Roy stood up, pushed his chair back and approached her.

"Gettin' an early start on the workday, I see," he said, sliding his hands into his rear pants pockets. He smiled wickedly at her. "Want some grub? Or are you too good to sit among the gents who still smell of yesterday's labors?"

"Stand away from me. It is you that I'm smelling, and the scent I am getting is skunk," Billie said, placing her fists on her hips.

"Why, you bi—" Roy began, but he stopped short of using the word.

He knew that he had to watch what he said and did for though Billie didn't know it yet, she had the upper hand.

"I'd watch what you call me," Billie said, her green eyes narrowing angrily. "Roy, I've more journals to check over, and then we have a bone or two to pick."

"What sort? Chicken or turkey?" Roy said, laughing as he tried to make light of what he suspected she already knew about his position in the company.

Billie turned on her heel and left the bunkhouse. She walked her horse back to the stable, removed its saddle, then went inside the house.

Feeling dirty from her encounter with Roy, she splashed her face clean at the water basin and then washed her mouth out as well.

The smell of bacon drew her to the kitchen, where she found her father's cook and maid, Sara, preparing her breakfast at the wood-burning kitchen stove.

"Sara, I'm not all that hungry," Billie said, her belly feeling too uneasy to even think of putting much food in it. "If you will, please just bring me a bowl of grits in the study. I'll eat something more substantial later. I plan to be home most of the day."

"You look so pale, Billie," Sara said in her slight voice, which matched her build. She was in her late fifties, with dark hair streaked with gray. She was petite with a pale skin and pretty, slightly slanted blue eyes.

"Are you all right, hon?" Sara said, taking a closer look at Billie.

"Not exactly, but it's nothing to worry about," Billie said, smiling. "It's just that I had no idea things were as confusing here as I'm finding them to be. The journals . . . the men . . . Roy. Altogether it's a pain in the neck, Sara."

Billie's gaze lingered on Sara for a moment. The woman had been a dutiful cook and maid for Billie's family for many years now and had grown close to them. Billie's mother had sent Sara along with Billie's father to Makah land in order for him to have some sort of civility, and she had kept him fed and the house clean.

Sara wiped her hands on her apron and placed a hand on Billie's cheek. "You have to eat to keep up your strength. You are taking on far more than you should since your father's death," she consoled. "Your mother would turn over in her grave if she knew the sorts of things you're doing. You know she didn't want you to have this kind of life."

Sara gazed at Billie's hair. "And your hair, Billie," she said with a huge sigh. "Lordy, your *hair*."

"I know," Billie said, taking Sara's hand affectionately. "My hair will grow back. But as for everything else? It all changed when Mother died, and then . . . then . . . Father, too. My life has been turned upside down. But I am a survivor. I will get through this all right."

"Why don't you sell out so we can both go back to Seattle?" Sara asked, easing her hand from Billie's. "I've never liked it here. It's too isolated. You're used to the hustle and bustle of city life."

"I have much to think over before I come to a final decision," Billie said, and in her mind's eye she saw the sculpted face of a handsome man. Although Proud Eagle surely could never feel anything for her but resentment, she wanted so much more.

She at least wanted to have a civil conversation with him. And last night she had dreamed of him embracing and kissing her.

Yes, she did have things on her mind that needed to be straightened out, that was certain.

"I always dreamed of being a teacher, or doing something with children," Sara said, a wistful look on her face. "But my parents didn't have money for my education to be one. I've done quite well bein' what I've been. Your parents always treated me like a jewel."

"You have a job for as long as you like," Billie said, hugging her. "You are all the family I have left, Sara."

"You're all I have, too, since my parents' passing.

You've been like my daughter," Sara said, returning the hug. "Please be careful with what you are doing. Going out to work with the men like you've been doing is dangerous. You know that your father took precautions when he was felling trees, and even that didn't stop him from . . ."

Sara's voice caught and she lowered her eyes.

"Yes, Sara, I know what you're saying," Billie said, placing a hand beneath Sara's chin and lifting it gently so that they could look into each other's eyes again. "And you can rest easy knowing that I don't believe I'll be going with the men again.

"But, as I said, I've lots to sort out. It begins today with me studying my father's journal. Perhaps something will come to light in his words that I haven't been able to figure out by studying his ledgers."

"I don't like Roy Clawson," Sara said, scowling. "He's a bad one, he is. Be careful around him, Billie. He's the sort to take advantage, especially of an innocent young lady like yourself. Without your father here to protect you, I—"

"Please stop worrying," Billie urged her. "I am much stronger than you realize, both mentally and physically. Roy Clawson isn't going to get away with anything."

Billie gave Sara another reassuring smile, then hurried to the study. She left the door ajar so that she could see or hear Roy if he came anywhere near.

She had brought her father's private journal to the study earlier and had hidden it behind the books in the massive bookcase. Now she went to a drawer in one of the tables, shuffled through a thick layer of papers, and withdrew a key that she had hidden there. She unlocked the bookcase, then reached behind the books and took out the journal.

Taking it back to the table, she built a fire in the fireplace and settled down in a leather chair before it.

She began reading, from page one, feeling her father in the words and envisioning so much of what he wrote about.

He had started this journal when he still lived in Seattle with Billie and her mother. There were so many entries about his feelings about his family, then later on, thoughts about how he had to make a decision of whether or not to stay in Seattle.

Billie choked up when she came to the part where her father had said his good-byes on the day he had left for land he had chosen near Eagle Bay.

He wrote about how he had hoped that Billie's mother would change her mind and accompany him there with their daughter, especially after he had described to her the sort of home he was building especially for the ladies.

Tears filled Billie's eyes when she read how her father broke down and cried on the steamer as he headed for this new land, new trees, and a new home.

Her father wrote about Sara, saying that she was his only salvation at that time. Her heart sank and her eyes widened.

"Sweet, sweet Sara, who warms my bed each night . . ." Billie read aloud his exact words.

The woman Billie had loved as much as she might a sister, or aunt, and had only moments ago embraced. Sara had been sleeping with Billie's father.

"No," she cried brokenly. She closed her eyes as she tried to block out the image.

Sara had always been so dutiful to Billie and her mother while living with the family in Seattle. Had she been his mistress even then?

"What am I to do?" she whispered, uncertain that she could be around Sara now that she knew the secret.

Sara had no one in the world now but Billie. If Billie were to send her away, where would she go?

Billie's mother and father had been estranged before her father had moved away and Billie had been aware that they had not shared a bed for many years. Somewhere in time, had her mother and father's love grown bitter? Had it been because of Sara?

Or had Sara taken the responsibility of a wife when Billie's mother gave it up?

"Oh, what am I to do?" Billie said, her voice breaking.

"Billie?"

The sound of Sara's voice out in the hallway made Billie's heart leap with alarm.

"Billie, I've brought you your grits and a cup of tea," Sara said, opening the door with the toe of her shoe. Her hands were filled with a silver tray, on which sat Billie's breakfast.

Billie hurriedly closed the journal, but not before turning down a corner of the page so that she could go back to it.

"Thank you," she murmured, rising to take the tray.

She tried hard not to behave differently, for she knew that Sara would notice the change and wonder about it.

Billie was not yet ready to confront Sara about this. She had to figure it out first, as best she could, by reading more of her father's journal.

Surely she would find the answers that she needed.

As Sara handed Billie the tray, her eyes met Billie's.

"What's wrong, honey?" she asked. "Why are you looking at me so strangely?"

Billie blinked and turned her face away. "I'm sorry, Sara. As I said earlier, I've lots on my mind, and lots to sort through."

"I understand," Sara said softly.

Billie spun around to face Sara. "Do you?" she asked, her eyes searching Sara's.

"What do you mean?" Sara asked, turning pale. "Billie, what's the matter? You've never acted this way before. Have I done something to trouble you?"

"I'm sorry, Sara," Billie said with a sigh. "Thank you for bringing the tray."

Sara gazed at Billie with a question in her eyes, then left the room in a flurry.

Billie sighed again, then sat down and picked up the bowl of grits, but she just couldn't eat anything right now, not after having just looked her father's lover in the eye.

"Father, Father," Billie whispered. "Why? You were so handsome. You could've had any woman you wanted. Why Sara?"

She set the bowl of grits back on the tray, then thumbed farther ahead in the journal, past the passage about Sara, and resumed reading.

She soon forgot her concerns about Sara when she came to entries about Roy Clawson and his relationship with her father. Everything her father wrote about Roy was negative.

Her father was concerned about Roy, about him being gone for days at a time on steamers to towns where he gambled and drank nonstop. Roy was letting him down; he was becoming worthless.

"And Roy is now borrowing against his partnership," Billie found herself reading aloud.

"Roy has already lost most of the business," Billie read. "I will have to watch and see what happens, but I'll have to make an important decision soon about Roy. Should I send him away and find someone more reliable?"

Billie was so caught up in reading about Roy and thinking about what it could mean that she didn't notice someone lurking outside the partially open door.

But suddenly she was aware of footsteps. She

looked guardedly toward the door, but saw no one. The sound stopped.

She shrugged and continued reading, but this time to herself.

Roy stood quietly in the corridor, pale from hearing what Billie had just read out loud about her father's feelings about him and his portion of the business. Roy realized that he had to work fast, or he would lose everything. Thus far he had managed to hang on by a thread. He had almost convinced Billie that he still had a good portion of the business in his name.

But now she knew too much.

And if she continued reading, and got to the entries that her father had written right before his death, she would soon know that he owned nothing of the company. He had gambled away everything.

He raced down the corridor and then outside toward the bunkhouse. He knew what had to be done—and soon.

Once Billie had the truth, then he'd have hell to pay!

Instead he would see that she met the devil first!

Billie closed the journal.

She gazed into the fire, stunned by all that she had discovered in her father's journal.

She had read of his affair with a woman she had

felt so close to for so long and of a partnership that had gone sour on him.

Billie shook uncontrollably when she thought of Roy.

Had Roy caused her father's death in order to gain full control of the company?

Had he the skills to convince the faithful lumberjacks that her father had died accidentally in order to persuade those same men to be as loyal to him?

"Oh, Lord—" Billie whispered, her voice breaking. "How can I prove *that*?"

She eyed the journal. Perhaps if she read more, she would find out what she needed to know. But for the moment she needed an escape. She needed to be away from all of this.

She needed . . .

Yes, oh, Lord, she needed someone to talk to— someone she could trust.

In her mind's eye she suddenly saw Proud Eagle.

Chapter Thirteen

Billie sat at her dresser, grimacing as she brushed her short hair. She still couldn't believe that she had cut her hair. In hindsight it was ridiculous to believe she could step into her father's vacant position. She was no longer that child who had loved standing in her father's shadow those long years ago, pretending she was the son he had wanted so badly.

At that time she would gladly have cut her hair if she'd thought it would please her father. She had always wanted to please him, in hopes of making him forget that she wasn't a son, but instead a dutiful daughter who adored him. And now she had cause to believe he didn't deserve any devotion she might have paid him.

"That was so long ago," she whispered as she continued to brush her hair. "I'm no longer that little girl hoping to please."

She knew things about him now that made her skin crawl, personal things, as well as business. Sara.

How could he have done such a thing as that? And how long had it been going on?

Had they slept together under the same roof as Billie's mother?

"Quit thinking about that," Billie ordered herself.

She slammed the brush down on the dresser. She would put that out of her mind, at least for now. She had made plans for today that excited her.

In her brief moments with Many Winds, when he had inadvertently cuddled next to her as she was taking him home on her horse, she had felt a strange, immediate bond with the child.

If she had not found him . . .

No! She wouldn't think about that. She *had* found him, and he was already back at school.

She had seen him arrive yesterday when she had been observing the school from a safe distance, well enough hidden that no one would realize she was there.

His father had delivered him, and she had seen no hesitation on Many Winds' part as they walked into the school. He was still limping, though, which meant that he was not yet totally well.

When Proud Eagle had wheeled around and begun riding away from the school, Billie had eased her horse farther back into the shadows to make certain that he wouldn't see her. She was afraid of being accused of spying, when, in truth, she only wanted to see if Many Winds was all right.

Now she heard boisterous laughter coming from

outside. She went to the window to investigate and saw several of the lumberjacks playing horseshoes during their idle time—time that she had "assigned" them. Until she had things sorted out in her mind about what she was going to do about the business as a whole, she had told the men to find something to do.

Roy Clawson had been her only problem. He had tried to usurp her authority by saying that she had no right to stop production. He insinuated that her father would despise what she was doing.

She had flatly told him that he had no choice but to do as she said. She knew that she had much more control of the business than he did. But she had not told him more than that. She didn't want him to know how much she had actually discovered.

She was glad that the men seemed to be accepting her position well enough. They seemed to be enjoying their time off. When they weren't outside playing horseshoes, they were pitching washers or playing poker. At night she could hear someone playing a harmonica.

Yes, all seemed well enough, and she was glad of it, since she still faced the terrible chore of telling the men that she didn't think she would continue with the lumber company.

First she had to find a way to tell Roy without him drawing a pistol and shooting her.

But now she had someone else on her mind.

Dressed in her riding clothes she hurried from her

room, down the beautiful staircase, and into the dining room, where a tall stack of steaming pancakes awaited her. She could smell the maple syrup and knew that Sara had warmed it just as she knew Billie liked it.

Sara.

Again, just thinking about that woman jarred Billie's senses.

No matter how hard she tried, she couldn't get past this woman's relationship with her father.

Hoping she could find some peace in her heart by escaping the house to take a picnic lunch to the school for herself and Many Winds, Billie spread butter between her pancakes, then poured syrup over them.

As soon as she took her first bite, it was easy to forget her hard feelings toward Sara for the moment. Sara was so good at what she did. No one could cook as well or keep house as beautifully.

But that side of Sara that she had kept hidden so well was something Billie found very hard to believe or accept. During the long years that Sara had been with the family, since Billie was five, Billie had seen nothing that would have led her to believe that Sara and her father had had a relationship.

When they had been in the same room together, Sara had treated Billie's father as her employer. She could not recall any sneaky, knowing smiles.

"Billie, I've got something for you," Sara said, interrupting Billie's thoughts.

Billie looked up to see Sara holding a huge platter of freshly made cookies.

"Your favorite, honey," she said, her eyes wavering as she gazed into Billie's. "Remember helping me make them when you were a child?"

"Yes, I remember loving to sprinkle the cinnamon on the top before you put them in the oven," Billie said, laying her fork aside. She could not help but get caught up in the sweet nostalgic feelings.

"Snickerdoodles," Sara said, smiling. "You love snickerdoodles so . . . so . . . I made them for you this morning."

"As a peace offering, no doubt," Billie said, finding it hard not to reach up and grab one of the cookies.

They *were* her favorite.

"Yes, in a way," Sara said. She set the tray on the table. She scooted a chair over close to Billie and sat down. "Honey, I know now that you know about me and your father. You must have read about it in his journal. I . . . knew . . . he had written it."

Sara swallowed hard, then said, "Billie, you've got to listen to my explanation."

"Yes, I did read it. And how can I be expected to understand that a woman I trusted and loved went behind my mother's back and slept with her husband?" Billie said.

She rose quickly from the chair and walked over to stand at a window. She noticed that no men were in sight, yet she could hear their muffled laughter.

She knew they were inside the bunkhouse, eating their own breakfast.

Her own appetite was gone.

Sara went to the window and stood beside Billie. She took one of her hands, but Billie quickly jerked away.

"I'm going to tell you, whether you want to listen or not," Sara said in a strained voice.

"How can you think anything you say will make a difference?" Billie asked, her eyes filled with resentment as she turned to Sara. "Sara, don't waste your time."

She started to walk away, but Sara was determined not to let her. She followed her and grabbed her hand. This time she wouldn't allow Billie to jerk it away.

"Let me go," Billie said, her eyes narrowing angrily. "Sara . . ."

"Your mother knew," Sara blurted out.

"Lord, no," Billie said, the color draining from her face. "Please don't tell me any more. I don't want to hear."

"Your mother not only knew, she encouraged it," Sara said, tears filling her eyes. "I don't believe you realize just how bad her health was. Her heart was so weak she didn't dare make love with her husband. When the doctor told her she must refrain from her marital duty because of the strain it would put on her heart, she was afraid that her husband would go to First Street and pay whores for time in their beds. She devised a way to keep him from doing that."

"No!" Billie said, succeeding in yanking her hand free. "You're lying to save face . . . to save your job."

"I'll leave if you wish, but first you must hear the whole story," Sara insisted. "Your mother brought me and your father together one evening when you were asleep. You were ten. I loved you so, Billie. I loved your mother so!"

"So much that you took over her responsibilities of keeping her husband satisfied," Billie said, finding this incredulous.

"It does sound horrible if you think of it in the way you are thinking," Sara said.

She turned and went and sat down at the table again. She plucked a cookie from the batch, stared at it, then put it back.

"I was stunned by your mother's decision," she said, tears shining in her eyes. "Your father was too, but your mother begged us to at least consider her suggestion. She loved your father so much she wanted him to have . . . everything a marriage offered, even if she had to bring another woman into it. Me."

"This is unbelievable," Billie said, throwing her hands in the air.

"But true," Sara murmured. She stood and went to Billie and gazed more deeply into her eyes. "Honey, it was awkward at first, but then it became a natural thing to do. I could not help but fall in love with your father, but he still loved your mother. They had a beautiful relationship."

"And you?" Billie asked, her voice breaking. "Surely you and Father had something you are not telling me. I know you, Sara. You wouldn't have allowed yourself to continue to be used unless love was exchanged between you and my father."

"Sometimes it is possible to love two women at the same time," Sara softly said. "Your father loved your mother so much, but yes, also me."

"When Father left to move here, was it to be with you?" Billie asked guardedly.

"No, Billie. He begged your mother to come with him," Sara said, her voice breaking. "He built this house for *her*. Yes, I would be a part of it, since I would still be working in the same capacity as I always had."

"How on earth did you manage to keep this a secret?" Billie asked grimly.

"It was done discreetly because we all loved you so much and wanted to protect you," Sara answered. "We were afraid that you would never understand."

"We," Billie gulped out. "There it is again. That word. We. It comes so easily for you to say it, as though you belong in my family."

"Your mother wanted it that way," Sara said, lowering her eyes. "At first I felt dirty, then the more your mother encouraged me the more I allowed myself to feel the wonders of a man's love for the first time in my life."

"I don't know if I can ever understand this, or give you any sort of blessing over what you have done," Billie said. She walked toward the kitchen. "I have been delayed long enough here. I have things to do."

"Can I help?" Sara asked.

Billie turned and glared at her. "Haven't you already done enough for my family?"

Sara lowered her eyes.

Billie felt some remorse. Sara had only been obedient to the wishes of Billie's mother and father. If Billie's mother felt at ease with such a suggestion, then why couldn't Billie accept it?

"I want to put together a picnic lunch," Billie said, her voice drawn. "If you want to help, I would appreciate it."

Sara's eyes lifted quickly, and in them Billie saw gratefulness.

"Who is the picnic for?" Sara asked, hurrying to the pantry and bringing out a wicker basket.

"I'm taking it to the school. I hope to have a picnic with Many Winds, the child I found and returned to his home at the Makah village," Billie answered.

"I know of the child," Sara replied. "He has often been seen watching the lumberjacks. Your father told me about him. Roy Clawson chased him off a time or two. When I saw the child, I didn't see how anyone could be cruel to him. I would be happy to get together something for him.

"I have a suggestion," she said.

"What?" Billie asked.

"Cookies," Sara said, her eyes twinkling. "Don't you think he would enjoy cookies more than anything else you could take for the picnic?"

"Snickerdoodles," Billie said, then smiled broadly at Sara. "Yes. The snickerdoodles you made for me. I can take them to the school."

"Perhaps you could give some to all the children," Sara said. "I made many more than what I brought to you on the platter."

"That's a wonderful idea," Billie said, hugging Sara without thought. Then she stepped quickly and awkwardly away from her.

"Please don't do that," Sara said, her voice breaking. "Please don't treat me as though I am poison. Billie, what I did, I did out of love for your mother. It is just by chance that I fell in love with your father. But it never took away from your father and mother's relationship. In fact, it strengthened it. They shared me, Billie. We all three shared a special love."

"I just don't know," Billie said. She turned her back to Sara and hid her face in her hands. "It is all so new to me, and so strange."

"In time, when you think it over, I hope you will understand and . . . forgive," Sara replied quietly.

She brought out a huge jar of the cookies from the pantry. "For now, let's concentrate on the children. I have never thought it was right for the Makah children to be put in that terrible boarding school."

"You know about it?" Billie asked.

"Yes, and I have often taken fresh-baked goods

to them," Sara answered. "But I never took them snickerdoodles. It was our private favorite between us, Billie, yours and mine."

"Well, today the children shall have a special treat, then," Billie said, helping to pack the basket. "Thank you, Sara."

"Thank you, Billie, for all of the love you've given me through the years—and I hope you will, again, in the future," Sara said in a shaky voice. "I love you no less than if you were my very own daughter."

Tears filled Billie's eyes and she flung herself into Sara's arms. "Forgive me for my harsh words to you today," she said. "Sara, you have always meant so much to me. I—I—could never hate you. Never."

"There, there," Sara murmured as she stroked Billie's back. "Child, I have missed you so much these past years after moving here. I had so hoped that your mother would change her mind and join us. But she just couldn't see living in such an isolated place. She had her friends and her millinery shop."

"Yes, she was loved by so many," Billie said, sniffling and wiping her nose with the back of a hand.

"Enough of this," Sara said, covering the cookies with a cloth. She handed the basket to Billie. "I believe you have a delivery to make."

Sara walked Billie to the door and watched her go to the stable for her horse and buggy. She was so glad when Billie turned to her, smiled, and waved.

Tears of relief spilled from Sara's eyes as she smiled and waved back.

Chapter Fourteen

As Billie pulled the horse and buggy up before the boarding school, she felt some apprehension about what she was about to do. What if she was regarded as an interloper because she showed interest in the Makah children? Would the headmistress think she was snooping?

But she was determined to earn Proud Eagle's trust so that she could apologize for what her father had done. In addition, she truly wanted to know Proud Eagle's son better, and to discover what had happened to his mother. She left the buggy and secured the horse's reins on the hitching rail.

She took the basket of cookies from the wagon and turned to go into the school, but stopped when she found Anna standing at the door, glaring at her.

"Good morning, Anna," Billie said, smiling. "It's nice to see you again."

"What are you doing here?" Anna huffed, her arms folded across her chest. "And what do you have there?"

"I've brought cookies for the children," Billie said. "And I was hoping for some private time with Many Winds now that he is well enough to be back at school."

"Why should I allow you to see him?" Anna asked, not budging.

"I'm sure you know that I'm the one who found Many Winds and took him home to his father," Billie answered. "And I recall you saying that children can leave the school for a while with family for picnics. Well, I'm not his family, but we are friends. May I, Anna?"

"And what makes you think he wants to be with you?" Anna said, moving toward Billie.

"I'm not certain he does, but I hope so," Billie said, holding the basket in her right hand and allowing the woman to approach her.

"But what is your interest in the child?" Anna asked.

"I haven't talked with him since I left him with his father," Billie said. "I only want a moment with him. I had planned to bring a picnic lunch just for the two of us, but instead I brought cookies for everyone."

Anna sighed as she gazed at the basket and then at Billie. "Well, all right," she said. She stepped aside and motioned toward the door. "Go on. I shall follow."

"Thank you," Billie said. She did not hesitate. She didn't want to give Anna the chance to change her mind. She preceded Anna into the schoolroom, where the children were sitting quietly at their desks, listening to their teacher as she explained what their next lesson would be.

Anna spoke briefly to the teacher, then motioned for Billie to come ahead to the front of the room.

By then the children had all turned to look at her, following her progress as she went to stand between the teacher and the headmistress.

"Children," Anna said, taking charge. "Billie Shaughnessy has brought something for you."

She nodded to Billie. "You tell them," she said, a sudden gentleness in her voice.

Billie stepped in front of the children, her eyes searching for Many Winds.

When she saw him sitting near to the back, he was smiling ear to ear. She smiled back at him.

Then she gave all of the children a warm smile and set the basket on the teacher's desk. "Yes, I have brought you something," she said, removing the cloth that covered the cookies. She brought one out for the children to see. "I've brought cookies for you."

She heard murmurs of excitement across the room.

"They are called 'snickerdoodle' cookies," Billie said, causing looks of puzzlement among the children.

"Yes, it's a strange name, but the taste is delicious," Billie explained. She turned to Anna. "May I?"

Anna nodded.

Billie moved from child to child, letting them reach into the basket. "Take two apiece," she instructed. "There are plenty."

It thrilled her to see the children taking the cookies, holding one in each hand, so proud.

"Go ahead," Billie encouraged. "Eat them. They are my favorite."

Anna came up after Billie had passed the basket around the room. "I've never heard of such a cookie," she said. "I smell cinnamon."

"Take one," Billie said, then smiled at the teacher. "You must have one, too."

Even Billie took a cookie and ate it along with everyone else. When the cookies were all gone, Anna went and whispered into Many Winds' ear about what Billie wanted to do. Billie saw a look of surprise enter the child's dark eyes.

"Yes, child, you can go with Billie for a while," Anna said, patting Many Winds on the shoulder.

Billie went to him. She winced when she saw that it still pained him to put his full weight on his foot, which was still somewhat swollen from the spider bite.

She took his hand and walked him out of the building, then ushered him over to the shade of a tree. "Wait here," she told him.

She brought a blanket from her buggy and spread it beneath the tree. She was glad that Many Winds didn't hesitate to sit down with her.

"I'm so glad you agreed to have some private time with me," Billie said.

"I'm glad you came," Many Winds said, smiling sweetly at her. "I haven't had a chance to thank you for finding me and taking me home to my father."

"I wish I had found you earlier," Billie said, stroking his long black hair. It was the same color as his father's, and surely the same texture.

She had never before appreciated long hair on a man, but after seeing Proud Eagle's, she had not been able to stop thinking about threading her fingers through it.

"I am all right now," Many Winds said. "Thank you. And my father and friends thank you."

"I hope to be able to talk with your father one day," Billie said.

"What about?" Many Winds asked, raising an eyebrow.

"Oh, just things," Billie said, knowing it was best not to bring up the true reason she needed to talk with Proud Eagle. She had much to make up to him, if only he would allow it.

"I am truly sorry about your father," Many Winds said, causing Billie's eyes to widen.

"You are?" Billie said, remembering what he had said the other day about him.

"More than once I followed your father and Roy Clawson to see what trees they would be cutting that day," Many Winds said solemnly. "I usually did not let them know that I was there. I hid. But one day,

I told them that they were cutting Makah trees. I told them to stop."

She was the one to be surprised now. She was amazed at this child's bravery. "And what did they say to you?"

"The man who calls himself Roy said 'scat brat' to me," Many Winds said. "And your father did not apologize for the other man's rudeness."

Billie sighed. She put her hand on Many Winds' tiny shoulder. "Well, *I* apologize for both Roy's and my father's rudeness. My father treated you badly, yet you seem remorseful that he is dead."

"Only because he was your father," Many Winds answered truthfully. "I like you. You are nothing like him."

"I hope not," Billie said, slowly shaking her head.

"Where is your mother?" Many Winds asked.

"Like my father, she is also dead," Billie replied. "She died a short while ago."

"Then you are alone in the world?" Many Winds asked, his eyes widening. "You have no family?"

"None," Billie murmured. "But I'm all right. I am coping."

"Coping?" Many Winds asked.

"Getting along." Billie smiled sadly.

"Then I am coping, too," Many Winds said somberly. "I have only my father. My mother and grandparents died when mud came down onto our homes. I miss them all. But I have my father and my dog, Snow. We were out fishing when it began to rain.

We . . . had just reached shore when the mud slide happened. It happened so quickly."

Tears came to his eyes. "It was because your father and his men cut trees too close to my village," he said, wiping a tear from his eyes.

"I am so sorry about your loss and that my father had such a part in it," Billie said, yet she knew that those were just words and words were never enough when a child's heart was hurting.

She again thought about the stripped land that she had found. She hoped that it was far enough back that it would not cause another mud slide. She would make sure that no more trees were cut from that area.

And now she knew the fate of Proud Eagle's wife. He must despise her. Even though she had brought his son safely home to him he could not even thank her.

"I miss my mother and grandparents very much, but they are in a better place now," Many Winds said. "Our people believe that when one's spirit leaves the body, some people come and meet you in the sky. They are waiting there to take you with them. That is why no Makah are afraid to die. I am not afraid. I know that when I die it will be my mother and grandparents who will be there for me to take me home with them in the heavens."

Billie was impressed by this child who spoke with the voice of an adult.

"You will make someone a good mother," Many Winds blurted out. Then he giggled as he gazed at her hair. "Except for your hair, you are a pretty woman."

"My hair?" Billie said. She ran her fingers through the tight ringlets. "Ah, yes. My hair. I do wish that I hadn't cut it."

"I have never seen a woman whose hair is as short, or as red," Many Winds said, still staring at her.

"Well, I can't change the color, but with time I can change its length," Billie said. "I am going to let it grow back, and one day it will be long again."

"I wouldn't want you to change its color," Many Winds said. "It is like flame . . . so pretty."

Suddenly Many Winds flung himself into her arms. "Thank you again for saving me," he murmured, then rose and limped back to the school, soon disappearing inside it.

Billie grinned when he stepped back to the door again and smiled, then gave her a last wave.

She waved and plucked the blanket up from the ground just as Anna came out with the empty picnic basket.

Billie took the blanket to the wagon and smiled at Anna. "Thank you for giving me some time with the children, especially Many Winds."

"The children, especially Many Winds, enjoyed it," Anna said. "Do come again."

"I shall," Billie said, then boarded the buggy and drove off.

Billie treasured the memory of the sweet hug from Many Winds. Now if only she could get some sort of positive response from his father! Because of her own father's greedy ways, she had much to make up to Many Winds, Proud Eagle, and their people.

And she would.

Somehow.

Chapter Fifteen

Concerned about Many Winds and his adjustment to the school, Proud Eagle went to see the classroom where the children were dutifully doing what they called their "numbers."

His eyes searched until he saw Many Winds, who seemed to sense his father's presence. He turned toward his father and surprised him with a wide, contented smile.

Proud Eagle's eyebrows raised. He couldn't understand how his son had adjusted so quickly, after so recently fleeing the school.

He had not begged to stay home again, but it had been in Many Winds' eyes and demeanor that he still did not want to be at school. That Many Winds seemed to be happy among his classmates at the moment made Proud Eagle glad, though suspicious.

"Good morning, Proud Eagle," Anna said. "I see you came to check on your son."

"I need to know that he is accepting that which is required of him," Proud Eagle said, looking down at

Anna. "It would not be good for him to harbor the same ill feelings."

"I don't believe you have to worry about that. As you can see, your son is content enough."

Proud Eagle looked back at Many Winds, who was doing his schoolwork.

"There is such a change in him," Proud Eagle said, surprised to see the studious side of his son. "Do you know what might have caused this difference in my son's behavior?"

Anna studied Many Winds, and then looked up at Proud Eagle.

"Perhaps I do," she said slowly.

"Then what is it?" Proud Eagle prodded.

"Come, let's talk in my office," Anna said. "We don't want to be a distraction to the children."

When they arrived at her office, Anna motioned toward a chair. "Please sit," she offered, which he did.

She sat down behind the wide oak desk. "The children had a visitor today. But I believe she came to be with Many Winds."

"She?" Proud Eagle said, leaning forward. "Who are you referring to?"

"Billie Shaughnessy," Anna said, immediately recognizing a difference in Proud Eagle's eyes. "She brought a picnic basket of cookies. She asked if she could give them to the children, and when I said that it was all right, she passed them around until all the children had two each."

"She did this?" Proud Eagle said, stunned by the

woman's change in personality. First she defied him as she stood with the lumberjacks, then she rescued his son, and now she brought cookies for the children.

"You said that you believe she came to be with Many Winds, yet she shared her gift of food with all of the children," Proud Eagle said, not understanding the white woman's behavior.

"Miss Shaughnessy handed the cookies out to the children, then requested some private time with Many Winds," Anna answered. "I saw no harm in it since I knew she was the one who found your son when he was lost. Many Winds was eager to see her. So I allowed it."

"And where did they go?" Proud Eagle asked, unable to stop wondering if Billie's actions were sinister. Perhaps it was to trick Proud Eagle and his people.

"Just outside in the shade," Anna replied. "Miss Shaughnessy spread a blanket, and she and your son sat and talked for a while. Your son seemed to enjoy her company. They've formed a quick bond."

"I am confused by all of this," Proud Eagle said, sighing as he gazed out the window into the bright sunlight.

He recalled the woman on the day she had defied him with a stubborn stare, then later after she had cut her hair short. Proud Eagle could not understand why a woman as beautiful as Billie Shaughnessy would want to look and behave like a man.

"I, too, was confused at first, but now I see she is a very nice woman," Anna said. "She seemed very sincere."

"What else do you know about her?" Proud Eagle asked cautiously.

"Her father was the rich lumber baron who recently died," Anna answered. "And except for one man's possible claim to it, Miss Shaughnessy now seems to have control of the business."

"The daughter," Proud Eagle said quietly to himself. He found himself relieved that the woman belonged to no one.

Although he was wary of her past actions involving the lumber, her behavior toward the children, especially his son, was commendable.

If Anna, who seemed critical of almost everything and everybody, saw goodness in Billie Shaughnessy, Billie must have some admirable attributes.

"I have yet to thank her for what she did for my son," Proud Eagle said. "When she brought him home, I had no time to thank her. I was only thinking about him."

And even though he believed he owed her gratitude, he knew that their relationship must not go any farther than that. She might be a woman who truly cared for children, but there was that nagging suspicion that she had done what she had as a ploy to get on Proud Eagle's good side.

"I must go now," Proud Eagle said.

Anna followed him outside, where he mounted his

horse, then nodded farewell to Anna, who returned the gesture.

Proud Eagle glanced at the window behind which sat his son. Many Winds seemed to be engrossed in his schoolwork.

"Come again," Anna called as Proud Eagle wheeled his horse around.

"I shall," Proud Eagle replied. He looked straight ahead as he rode in the direction of the tall mansion that housed perhaps the most beautiful and intriguing woman that he had ever encountered.

Chapter Sixteen

Thunder rumbled in the distance. Dark clouds rolled across the heavens, like tempest waves on the ocean. There was already the smell of rain in the air, but that would not deter Proud Eagle's determination to speak to Billie Shaughnessy.

With his chin held high, Proud Eagle rode onward. He fought off the knowledge that there were other reasons why he wanted to come face-to-face with the flame-haired woman. He needed to discover whether or not she was true in her behavior toward his son or if it was all an act to gain something for herself. Whites had used children before to gain what they wanted.

But deep down, where trust lay like a balm to his senses, he wanted to believe that Billie had a good heart.

As Proud Eagle came past a break in the trees that gave him a clear view of the three-story mansion, he stopped for a moment. He looked from window to window, wondering which room was the woman's.

He had always been amazed at a home that required so many rooms, whereas he had all that he needed in his one-story, five-room longhouse.

Why did a man need to build such a monstrosity? Was it for the illusion of power? And what did living in such opulence really mean? After a woman grew used to living in such a place, could she really understand the way the Makah lived?

He snapped his reins against his black stallion's rump and rode out into the open and across a straight stretch of land toward the mansion.

Out of the corner of his eye he saw movement at the bunkhouse. It was Roy Clawson. He stopped to glare at Proud Eagle, then hurried toward the mansion.

Proud Eagle ignored the bald and obese man and rode on toward the mansion. He would not let the man interfere with what he must do.

He did not make it a habit of coming on this land that had been claimed by the whites he deplored. He always felt as though their evil was transferring to him when he was near them.

Roy positioned himself before the house, and Proud Eagle could hardly stand thinking that he might have to speak with him.

Thunder rumbled much closer now, causing Proud Eagle's thoughts to stray. Mud slides. Ever since he had lost so many loved ones in that one horrible mud slide, he had been worried about another. Now he needed to return home to his people, to prepare them for whatever might happen. He stopped a few feet from Roy, who still stood at the foot of the steps that led up to the front door. A sneer was on his fat face.

Proud Eagle found it difficult even to speak to him, much less explain why he was there. It was hard to tolerate the dishonest man, who would remove all Makah from the land, if he could.

Roy folded his arms across his chest in an open act of defiance. Proud Eagle slowly dismounted, then stood with his reins in hand as he stared back at him.

"Step aside, white man," Proud Eagle said, dropping his reins. "I am here to see Billie Shaughnessy."

"Over my dead body," Roy growled. "Scat, Injun. You ain't welcome here. I don't want you spreading your fleas and lice here."

Totally insulted, Proud Eagle wanted to hit the man, but he knew that he must refrain from violence. He became aware of the lumberjacks standing outside the bunkhouse, their hands resting on their holstered pistols as they watched what was transpiring between him and Roy.

Needing to put space between himself and this man who had the soul of the devil, Proud Eagle knew that—for now—it was best to leave. He did not want to do something that might cause his people much distress.

Proud Eagle fisted his hands at his sides and stood there for a moment longer, returning Roy's glare, then angrily mounted his horse.

Fighting off the desire that grew like wildfire

within him, to put the white man in his place once and for all, Proud Eagle wheeled his horse around and rode off at a hard gallop.

He felt foolish now for having come to this place for any reason. He vowed never to come again.

A fierce flash of lightning overhead in the darkened sky made him flinch.

The smell of rain was strong, and as he looked out to sea, he saw that the rain was quickly approaching land.

He pushed his horse to go faster and headed for home. "Where I belong!" he shouted aloud, feeling like a fool for trying to see her. When the face of the flame-haired woman came into his thoughts, he quickly shook it away.

Proud Eagle leaned low over his horse, his hair flying in the wind, as he felt the first raindrop on his face. He knew that it was one of many more to come.

With such dark clouds building overhead and the rumble of rolling thunder, he knew that they were in for a storm that could be as bad as the one that had taken so many lives!

Chapter Seventeen

"Billie?" Sara's soft voice called Billie's name from outside the library door, which was situated at the back of the house on the first floor. Billie's attention was jerked away from her father's journal. She had been so absorbed in reading the terrible accounts about Roy and comforted by the warm and wonderful fire in the fireplace that she had not noticed the approaching storm. Only now was she aware of the lightning flashing through the tall windows.

"Billie, I think you should listen to what I have to tell you," Sara persisted, through the door.

Hearing Sara's urgent tone, Billie placed a bookmark between the pages and laid the journal aside on a nearby table and hurried to the door.

"Billie, I think you should know that the Indian chief was just here and Roy ordered him away," Sara blurted out as Billie opened the door. "I watched from the parlor window. The chief had dismounted and I believe he wanted to come to the door, but Roy wouldn't allow it."

"What?" Billie gasped, feeling the color drain from her face.

"He's gone now," Sara said. "I just thought you should know that Roy did this."

"Yes, I should be told. Only I wish you had come earlier and told me he was here," Billie said, hurrying past Sara, hoping she could catch a glimpse of him. She looked at Sara over her shoulder. "But thank you, Sara, for telling me."

"It all happened so quickly," Sara said. She flinched when there was a loud crack somewhere close to the house, as though a tree might have just been struck by lightning.

"Goodness gracious, we're in for a fierce storm— like the one a few years back right after your father started cutting trees in the area," Sara said, shuddering. "I'll never forget that night. I didn't think it would ever stop raining."

Billie's insides churned as she heard several more claps of thunder and the howling of the wind.

She couldn't help but worry about mud slides, and now she knew that Proud Eagle had just ridden away and was out in this weather.

She broke into a run and rushed out onto the porch just as Roy was climbing the stairs to the house.

"Just you stop right there," Billie said, placing her fists on her hips. "Sara told me what you did. Why did you chase Proud Eagle off?"

Roy nodded at her. "Step aside, Billie Boy. Cain't you see we're in for a storm and a half?"

Billie watched as large drops fell on the ground, scattering as they made contact with the dry earth. She saw several drops pool on Roy's bald head.

Then she stared heavenward. Dark, billowing clouds were rolling in. "I haven't seen such clouds in years," she said, her voice breaking. "Once in Seattle . . ."

"Billie Boy, I don't care to hear you reminiscing about Seattle," Roy said, brushing past her.

Billie grabbed him by a wrist.

He glared dangerously at her. "Let me go," he said in a low hiss, his gray eyes flashing.

"Not until you hear what I have to say," Billie hissed back, her eyes flickering with anger.

"Well, then say it," Roy said, yanking his wrist free.

He flinched as another flash of lightning lit the dark clouds and more raindrops fell in large pools on the ground.

"How dare you keep Proud Eagle from seeing me," Billie said icily. "Who do you think you are?"

"I'm looking after you, that's all," Roy said sarcastically. "It's what your pa would want. You're nothing but a defenseless woman who needs a man to keep her safe. Well, Billie Boy, whether or not you like it, I'm your man."

"Never," Billie said. "Now tell me what Proud Eagle said."

"I already told you," Roy said, spitting over his shoulder. "He came to see you."

"Then why didn't you inform me that he was here?" Billie asked.

"Because the savage had no business here, or anywhere near this place, especially not in our home," Roy said tightly.

"Did I hear correctly?" Billie said, her eyes widening. "Did you just say 'our' when referring to this house?"

Roy's eyes narrowed angrily. "Billie Boy, I don't want to discuss this any further with you. I've got things to do."

"Like lie to me and cheat?" Billie said, brushing on past him. She opened the door and started to go in the house, but stopped. "Roy Clawson, I was going to wait a while to let you know this, but now's as good a time as any. I've read enough of my father's private journal to know that you have no rights at all to this land or house. My father left nothing out when he wrote of your gambling ways and what you lost because of it."

"I always get back what I lose," Roy snarled.

"Not this time," Billie said. "You gambled away the portion of the business that once was yours. You honestly don't have a pot to pee in. Now try to lie your way out of that one."

"You're wrong," Roy growled out. "And hear me well when I say this, Billie Boy—you're getting way too big for your breeches. You'd better watch yourself. I have the men on my side. Except for pretty little Sara, you are in this all alone. Watch your back, Billie Boy. Watch your back."

"You are actually threatening me?" Billie gasped.

"No, not threatenin', tellin'," Roy said, then bullied his way into the house.

Billie could not help but be somewhat afraid. She realized that it was Roy who was feeling threatened. She was in charge here. For now, she would let things slide.

Chilled to the bone, she stayed outside for a moment to watch as the rain fell from the heavens in what seemed solid sheets. Shuddering, Billie rushed inside the house and closed the door behind her.

As she was on her way back to the library, to get warm by the fire and continue reading her father's journal, she saw that the study door was slightly ajar.

She crept over and silently opened it a little farther. She was shocked to see Roy taking a picture from the wall behind her father's desk, revealing a safe behind it.

She watched, wide-eyed, as he skillfully maneuvered the combination and soon had the door wide open.

What was so troubling, but not surprising to her was that he hadn't told her about a second safe. He had purposely kept her in the dark.

She watched him riffle through papers in the safe, then pull out a single sheet.

Before she could say anything, he had struck a

match and was burning the document over a large ashtray.

"Stop!" Billie cried as she ran into the room and grabbed the burning piece of paper out of his hand. Only one corner survived but it was enough for her to see that it had been her father's will.

"I'll burn the journals next," Roy said, snickering. "You'll have no proof that your father left me nothing."

"You're a little late, don't you think?" Billie said, dropping the will into an ashtray, watching it burn down to ash. "I already know everything. You burning the will or journals will mean nothing."

"It will be your word against mine," Roy warned, his right hand resting on a holstered pistol at his waist. "If you know what's good for you, Billie Boy, you'll hand over my share right now. To hell with the gambling debts. I've worked them off a hundred times over alongside your father."

"My word will have much more weight than that of a sleazy, cheating gambler like you," Billie said, inching her way to the back of the desk as Roy scoffed at her.

In another moment she quickly opened a desk drawer and pulled out a tiny pearl-handled derringer. She aimed it at Roy. "You get out of here, Roy, and don't ever threaten me again. If you do, I'll see to it that you are locked up behind bars. In the meantime, you're going to help me get things in order around here as far as the lumberjacks are concerned. I'm closing down the business."

"You expect me to do anything for you now?" Roy said. He threw his head back in a fit of laughter.

He then looked somberly at her. "You'd best think about all of this before actin'," he warned. "You're going to be puttin' a lot of men out of a job. They won't be happy 'bout it. I'd hate to think what they might do."

"I don't believe they will do anything to harm me," Billie answered. "They all respected my father too much."

"Your father is dead," Roy said, chuckling. "So who do you now think the men will side with? Good ol' Roy, that's who, especially if I can guarantee them their jobs."

"Like I said, Roy, you have a choice to make," Billie said, shrugging. "You do as I say now, or you'll pay later."

Roy went to the window and looked up into the sky. "Comin' down like cats and dogs, but I ain't stayin' here with you any longer. I'll be out in the bunkhouse with the guys."

She watched him leave, then went to the window and saw him run through the rain to the bunkhouse, soon disappearing inside.

She stared into the pouring rain. She couldn't remember seeing it rain this hard in her entire life, and while living in Seattle, she'd seen plenty of rain. It was building up into large pools on her lawn, and rushing from the hillside at the far side of the yard. It was making deep gullies in its wake.

"There could be another mud slide at the village," she whispered, shivering at the thought.

She would never forget the pain in Many Winds' voice as he recalled the mud slide that took so many of his family and others in the village.

What if this rain caused another one? Who would die this time?

She would not allow herself to think any more about that possibility . . .

"God a'mighty, look at that rain," one of the men said as Roy came into the bunkhouse, soaked to the bone.

"Forget the rain," Roy grumbled, flicking raindrops off his scalp. "We've got other worries."

"What sort?" one of the men asked. The others crowded around Roy.

"Billie Boy, that's what," Roy said, his eyes gleaming. "She just told me that she's taking away all my shares in the business. Now you'll have a lady boss, one hundred percent. What kind of a man works under a woman?"

He was lying through his teeth, and he wasn't planning to tell them that she was going to give up the business—that these men would have to look for work elsewhere.

That wasn't the way Roy wanted it. He wanted the

business. He needed the trees in order to make enough money to start over. He told himself that he had the gambling under control, he just needed enough cash to buy back his shares. Only Billie was standing in his way.

And he wanted Billie dead.

"I've been doing a lot of thinking, and I don't see much wrong in her being our boss," one of the men said, causing Roy's eyes to darken with anger. "And something else, Roy. I want my job, and if we leave it up to you, you'd gamble everything away. We know what happened to your shares. She's nice. She's fair. No. I've decided that I won't do anything to stop her."

He turned to the rest of the men. "Are you with me or with Roy?" he shouted.

"With the lady," the men said almost in unison.

One of the other men stepped up to Roy. "And hear me well, Roy. You'd best do nothin' to make us lose our jobs, or you'll have hell to pay. Do you hear? You'll pay. We've all talked this over. We're for who'll guarantee our wages, and Roy, that ain't you."

"You're a fool," Roy spat. "The truth is she's sellin' out. Do you hear? None of us will have a job."

"You're a liar," one of the men said. "Roy, we're sidin' with the lady. If you want to work side by side with us, that'd be fine. You're good at what you do. Your problem is gambling. It's time for you to see what's best for you, Roy, and gambling ain't it."

"I'm tellin' the truth when I say she's sellin' out," Roy said, looking from man to man. "What can I do to make you believe me?"

"Nothin'," the men said, turning away.

Disgruntled, Roy left the bunkhouse. Although it was raining hard, he got his horse and rode away. He looked over his shoulder at the lights in the mansion.

"Billie Boy, you're going to pay for this," he whispered. "No one gets the best of Roy Clawson. Especially not you, you redheaded witch!"

Chapter Eighteen

After struggling for hours with her racing thoughts—wondering why Proud Eagle had come to see her and cursing the weather for stopping her from following him—Billie had finally fallen asleep. But she had been awakened by the incessant thunder and lightning. Realizing that it was still raining hard, she went to the window to peer at the storm. It looked like it might be letting up, but she couldn't help but worry about what such a rainfall could do where trees had been felled, leaving the earth barren and vulnerable. Before she had gone to bed, Billie had seen deep gullies all across her yard, especially on the slight hill on the one side.

The lumberjacks would be given duties, all right, but not to cut trees. She would ask them to work with the earth, to fill the gullies and quickly plant new trees there in order to get a root system going in the ground as quickly as possible.

Billie laid back down, but just as she started to

drift off a strange sort of rumbling made her sit up quickly in her bed.

Her eyes widened as the rumbling persisted, and her bed shimmied and shook from whatever was happening.

Her heart pounding, Billie jumped out of bed and went to the window again. She held aside the sheer curtains and saw that the sky was lightening along the horizon and the rain had stopped.

What she had heard was not thunder but something else—something even more ominous.

Suddenly the wind picked up and a sound was carried from the direction of the Makah village. Goose bumps raced across Billie's flesh and her face drained of color. People were wailing. Had the rumbling sound been another mud slide?

"Lord, please, no," Billie whispered aloud.

She hurried out of her gown, then yanked on her riding breeches, shirt, and boots.

Without stopping to brush her hair, she ran outside and saddled her horse.

She ignored the lumberjacks who had come outside to see what was happening. They watched her silently as she rode from the house.

Billie's pulse raced when she thought about what she might find at the village. Had history repeated itself? Would they hold her responsible, since it was her father and Roy who had felled the trees close to the Makah village again?

"Please don't let Proud Eagle be harmed," she

prayed as she gazed up at the heavens, where a beautiful orange glow came from the rising sun. "Please don't let anyone be hurt."

She rode harder along the shore, watching the waves lash angrily. The wind had not ceased its angry wail, carrying the cries of the Makah people.

"Father, oh, Father, what have you done?" she cried to the heavens.

Tears streaming down her cheeks, Billie realized that the wailing of the people had suddenly stopped. She could hear voices, anxious and loud. And she realized that she was almost to the village. She hoped that she would be in time.

Her eyes widened as the village came into view. Her heart sank when she saw that a mud slide had partially covered some homes.

Chills ran up and down her spine when she saw a woman being pulled free of the muddy debris, then hugged desperately by a man who Billie assumed was her husband.

Afraid that someone might be dying beneath the mud, Billie rode harder, until she entered the village. She dismounted and ran over to the muddy mess.

She fell to her knees, and with her bare hands, began digging alongside several Makah women and men who were desperately trying to reach someone.

"Why are you here?"

An angry voice caused Billie's heart to skip a beat. She knew whose voice it was and she was actually afraid to look. She was afraid to stop digging. One moment longer covered by the mud and someone would certainly die.

She flinched when a hand gripped her wrist and pulled her to her feet.

Her eyes wavered as she found herself gazing into Proud Eagle's angry eyes. She gulped.

"Please let go," Billie choked out. "I heard the rumble from my home. I was afraid this might have happened. I came as quickly as I could to help."

"You are not wanted here," Proud Eagle said, angrily dropping his hand from her wrist.

He nodded toward her horse. "Go. Go to your home. Leave my people alone. Your father is to blame for what has happened today. And you are guilty as well of having interfered in the harmony of my people. When harmony is broken, illnesses, unsuccessful hunts, poor salmon runs, and now another mud slide come. Your family is responsible. Leave."

"No, I won't go. I can't," Billie said, her voice breaking. "I had nothing to do with what has happened. I've wanted to apologize to you about so many things that my father and Roy have done. Please allow me to prove that my heart is in the right place, that my intentions are pure. Please let me help make wrongs right."

She felt his wrath by the heat in his eyes. And his words caused an ache in her heart.

But she had to prove her point, that though she

was her father's daughter, she was vastly different from him.

She gazed at him a moment longer, then slowly sank to her knees. With her bare hands she once more began digging alongside the others, until her fingers began to feel raw, and then almost numb.

She was determined to make Proud Eagle understand. She cared deeply for humanity. And she was not prejudiced against anyone whose skin color was different from hers.

Proud Eagle was stunned by her disobedience. She was back on her knees, her fingers clawing frantically at the earth, the mud soaking into the knees of her breeches. He realized that she was serious about wanting to help his people.

Proud Eagle brought Billie a digging tool. He dropped to his own knees and began digging alongside her.

Surprised and grateful for the tool, Billie couldn't believe that Proud Eagle was digging beside her. She hoped he believed her intentions were true after all. Just maybe they could be friends . . .

When she was near him, something inside her heart warmed, and in the pit of her stomach, she felt a strange sensation.

She had never been in love. Could this be how it felt?

She knew this wasn't the time to be thinking about anything but saving lives. She continued to dig as people were freed from the mud on all sides of her, all of them alive, but weakened and coughing as they struggled for breath.

Thankfully, no one had died. They were rescued in time. The main damage was done to the homes. It was obvious to Billie that longhouses could withstand most weather, but not the weight of mud. She quickly followed Proud Eagle to the next mud-covered longhouse.

She briefly thought about how she had formed a bond with Many Winds that day when she had found him.

Strange how it could happen, but she actually believed that the same sort of bond was forming between herself and the child's father.

Chapter Nineteen

The digging was finished now that everyone was ac-
counted for. Billie rose to her feet, exhausted.

She didn't even look at Proud Eagle as she stum-
bled, weak-kneed, toward her horse, for his looks
had said it all every time she had glanced at him.

Although she was trying hard to prove that she
was sorry about all that had happened, the resentment was still in Proud Eagle's eyes, as well as those
of his people.

Wanting only to escape from this place where she
was thought of as an enemy, Billie mounted her
horse and rode out of the village.

Tears filled her eyes at her knowledge that no matter what she did, she could never undo what her
father had done to these people. Perhaps once they
saw that she was shutting down the business, the
Makah would finally believe that her heart was in
the right place. Until then she would stay away from
them and especially Proud Eagle.

Although she could not fight the feelings she had

for him in her heart, she would have to force herself to forget him.

Along the shore, the ocean was calm now, the sun beaming. Billie dug her heels into the flanks of her horse and enjoyed the ride. She had grown fond of this land that seemed to have grown out of the sea, but she would leave the mansion and everything it stood for and return to Seattle.

She would not sell the mansion, for fear that it would only bring more whites to the land.

Yes, she would abandon the mansion. Her father's dream would die, a dream that had been shadowed by greed.

Suddenly aware of a horse coming up behind her, Billie looked quickly over her shoulder. She gasped to herself when she saw Proud Eagle.

She was confused by his arrival and afraid that he might still have hard words for her that would sting her heart. Yet the look on his face was not the same as it had been a short while ago at the village.

Now there was a look of kindness in his eyes, and his bare, muscled shoulders were relaxed.

"Wait!" Proud Eagle shouted, waving at Billie. "I have much to say to you."

Sighing heavily, she wheeled her horse around and waited for Proud Eagle until he came alongside her strawberry roan.

"What is it?" Billie dared to ask.

"I am grateful for what you did today, as well as what you did for my son," Proud Eagle said, searching her eyes. "For someone who portrayed herself as my enemy, you are proving yourself, time and time again, to be otherwise."

"I have never been anyone's enemy—except perhaps Roy's—and I don't want to be," Billie murmured. "Proud Eagle, I investigated and found that my father and Roy were wrong about so many things. I want to make things right. Please give me a chance."

Proud Eagle saw the sincerity in her eyes and believed that she was being honest. He wanted her in his arms, a feeling he had been fighting since that first moment when she had defied him with flashing eyes and bitter words. Now he brought his horse closer and pulled her from her horse to his.

Wet with mud, Billie slipped from his lap and fell clumsily to the ground.

She lay there in the mud, slightly stunned and gazing questioningly up at Proud Eagle as he dismounted.

His lips quivered and he broke into a slow, infectious smile, causing Billie to smile back. Then they both dissolved in a fit of laughter.

"Yes, I know I look a sight," she gasped, "but you do, too. You have as much mud on you as I do. You just aren't lying in it."

Proud Eagle's smile faded as he knelt beside Billie.

"Will you come with me?" he asked, searching her eyes.

Billie's own laugher faded as she gazed into his dark eyes. "Where?" Billie asked.

"Trust me?" Proud Eagle said, taking her by the hand, helping her up from the ground.

Billie was caught up in something very new to her—feelings of wonder for a man. His handsomeness caused her insides to feel deliciously warm.

Proud Eagle held her hand as he led her to her horse then helped her into her saddle. He went to his own black steed and mounted, then snapped his reins and rode off at a lope. Wanting nothing more than to be with him now, Billie snapped her own reins and rode next to Proud Eagle. They made a sharp turn to the left, which took them into a valley of tall trees. They rode onward for some time until the shine of the ocean was once again visible. Billie followed Proud Eagle out of the trees, where he soon drew up on the beach.

"It is a good place to wash in private," Proud Eagle said, dismounting. "We are far from our homes, especially from prying eyes."

Suddenly somewhat apprehensive about what he was leading her into, and feeling very vulnerable, Billie hesitated before dismounting.

"You can trust me," Proud Eagle said, reaching up for her.

Believing that she really could trust him, Billie eased into his arms and slid from her horse.

When her feet were on solid ground, so close to Proud Eagle that their breaths mingled, Billie felt the weakness return to her knees. However, this time it was because a wonderfully handsome Indian chief was gazing down at her with a searing look in his eyes. Her heart wanted his arms around her, and his lips on her own.

But she was disappointed to find that he had other things on his mind.

"You had best remove your boots before we swim," Proud Eagle said, desperately trying to control his heartbeat and a deep yearning to kiss her.

"And my . . . clothes?" Billie asked, shocking herself that she would even suggest it.

"No. Your clothes need bathed as much as you," Proud Eagle said, resisting the temptation to reach over and help her undress.

He hungered to see her body, the curves so well defined in the mud spattered clothes. But he knew that she was a woman who would not hurry into anything, especially taking her clothes off in the presence of a man who only recently had been a total stranger and perhaps in her eyes, her enemy.

"Yes, they do," Billie murmured, blushing at the knowledge that she would have totally undressed, had he suggested it.

This was new to her—this want, this need, of a man. But she did want him. She wanted to know every nuance of him.

She slid her boots off and he removed his moccasins, then laughing, they ran into the ocean together and began to swim.

Proud Eagle reached out for her and drew her close. She twined her arms around his neck as they gazed into each other's eyes, her heart thumping wildly.

He brought his lips down to hers, his arms holding her tightly, their bodies straining together hungrily. Kissing him was like entering paradise.

Stunned by the sweetness of the kiss, and knowing now that he had finally found a woman who could still the yearnings he had had since the death of his beloved wife, Proud Eagle leaned away from her. He was unsure whether this could ever work, since they were of a different skin color and her father had been his worst enemy.

Proud Eagle slowly ran his fingers through her wet red ringlets. "You should not have cut your hair," he said huskily. "Why did you?"

"When I first came from Seattle and buried my father, I felt inclined to finish what he had started here," Billie answered quietly. "I wanted to finalize his dream."

She lowered her eyes, swallowed hard, then looked up at him again. "I cut my hair so that I would fit in better with the men," she said softly. She would never tell him the whole truth behind her cutting her hair, that she had done it to spite him after he had gazed at its wonderful length.

"I did it without thinking about what I wanted, that I might not want to follow in my father's footsteps after all," she went on. "It did not take long for me to regret not only having cut my hair, but also the trees that I know now belong to your people."

"And so you do know this, do you?" Proud Eagle said solemnly. "You know that your father went against the treaty stating that portions of the land belonged to the Makah?"

"Yes, I know," Billie said, swallowing hard. "Why did you allow him to cut those trees?"

"My people come first in all things," Proud Eagle said stiffly. "Were I to go against whites, even though I was within my right to do so, it would come back to my people twofold. As long as your father and his men came only so far, then I would allow it. It was only recently—before your father died—that I knew something had to be done. I was making plans when I heard of your father's death."

He drew her closer. "I am sorry about your father," he said. "No matter how scheming a man he was, he was still your father."

"I never knew that side of him," Billie said honestly. "When he cut trees near Seattle, I thought it was all legally done. Perhaps even then it wasn't. Maybe that was why he fled."

"Enough talk now about your father," Proud Eagle said softly. "Swim with me. I have a special place for you."

Billie smiled and dove into the water with Proud Eagle, and they swam side by side. Then he stopped and held her hands at a spot where she could stand on the bottom of the ocean.

He swam a short distance away from her, then dove into the water. When he surfaced, he was carrying something that was so lovely it took Billie's breath away. He held it out to her.

"What is this?" she asked, as he placed it in her hand. "It's so tiny and beautiful."

"It is a zebra mussel," Proud Eagle replied, watching her study it. "It is a shellfish that attaches itself to rocks far beneath the surface."

"It is so pretty," Billie murmured, still studying it. Then something at her left side drew her attention. "My Lord, look!"

What she was seeing were baby hair seals, emerging from a cave that stretched out into the water.

"The high tide of this time of year washes the autumn births of hair seals out of the caves," Proud Eagle said, watching the small things battling the water. "It is the surest sign of winter's approach."

He turned to Billie again. "Would you like to see the seals up close inside the cave?" he asked.

"Yes, I would love to," Billie said.

"Tomorrow?" Proud Eagle said. "I need to get back home today to help my people."

"As I need to go to talk with Roy," Billie said. "I have to set things straight with him once and for all. After today, he will know where he stands and that he'd best abide by my decisions."

"Decisions?" Proud Eagle asked, raising an eyebrow.

"Yes, I've made an important decision and it's time that the lumberjacks know what it is," she said, walking out of the water with Proud Eagle. She leaned down and placed the tiny mussel back in the water, then pulled on her boots and went to her horse.

"I'll explain it all to you tomorrow," Billie said, mounting her horse.

"Yes, tomorrow," Proud Eagle said. "Meet me at my village at midday?"

"Yes, at midday," Billie agreed. He reached over, wrapped his arm around her waist, drew her close, and kissed her.

After he released her, Billie managed despite her awestruck state to get her horse to move. As she rode toward her home, she felt as though she was floating above the saddle.

"This is really happening!" she shouted to the heavens. "Father? Mother? Do you see? Do you see how happy I am?"

When she arrived home, she found herself the target of Roy's laughter and knew why. She was still soaking wet, with mud lodged in her boots.

She put her horse in the corral, then went to face Roy.

"Like I said earlier, Roy, it's over," she said tightly. "There will be no more cutting of trees. It's important that you know I mean business. Pack up your things, Roy."

"You fool," Roy screeched. "I followed you. I saw you helping the Makah. And now you are going to let them trick you into not cutting trees? Your father would disown you, Billie. Disown you!"

"Perhaps," Billie said, standing her ground. "I just

know that the Makah have been taken advantage of, sad to say, by my father and those in his employ. In truth, Roy, you and the men are responsible for what happened today, and you know it. You had better be glad that none of the Makah people died in the mud slide. Both you and my father purposely crossed boundary lines. You went against treaties. Haven't the Makah already suffered enough? You had best be off this land by sundown.''

"You are actually siding with the enemy?" Roy shouted.

"You've got it wrong, Roy. *You* are the enemy," Billie said, her hands on her hips.

"We'll see about that," Roy growled as he turned away from her with a glare that made Billie's skin crawl.

She shivered involuntarily and went inside the house.

She watched from a window as Roy went into the bunkhouse. She hated to think what he might tell the men, or what he might do to retaliate.

She could not help but be uneasy.

Roy gathered the men around him in the bunkhouse. He looked from one to the other. "Well, the time that I expected has come. Billie Boy just gave me my walking papers. Gents, you'd best believe that you're next. It's over, men. It's the truth. You gotta believe me this time. You'll have to find jobs elsewhere, unless . . .''

"Unless what?" one of the men said.

"Unless you side with me and do as I say," Roy answered, with a gleam in his eye. "It's time to make plans. Those who side with me are guaranteed a job. There ain't no way in hell that witch is going to order me around. I'm here to stay. I'm here to cut trees. Who's with me?"

There was a strained silence, then, one by one, the men reluctantly agreed. They all knew how hard it would be to find a decent lumberjacking job again, after having worked with Theodore Shaughnessy and Roy Clawson. They had been chased out of Seattle and now there was no place else to run.

Roy smiled wickedly. "When she comes out to tell you the news, act as though you didn't already know. Then leave the rest to ol' Roy."

His throaty laugh filled the bunkhouse, making some of the men cringe and wonder about the sanity of Roy Clawson. But for now none of them had any choice.

Chapter Twenty

The sky was a brilliant turquoise blue overhead. The sun was casting a golden sheen on the water as Billie rode in Proud Eagle's canoe toward the cave.

It was such a beautiful day, it was hard to even envision a day like yesterday, when rain came from the heavens, it seemed, in buckets.

Billie wouldn't allow herself to dwell on the mud slide and the havoc it had wreaked at the Makah village. She was too happy to be with Proud Eagle.

It seemed so unreal, at times, to know that things had changed between them to something wonderful so quickly. She would never forget their kiss and the rapture of him enfolding her within his powerful arms.

Today his people had watched her board his canoe with bitter expressions. She hoped they didn't think that she was tricking their chief into giving up more of their land and trees in order to increase her wealth.

When she returned from this excursion with Proud

Eagle, she would break the news to the men who had worked dutifully at her father's side.

She hated to destroy their livelihood, especially for those whose families in Seattle or other small towns along Puget Sound awaited the arrival of money each month.

But she had no choice. She detested what the business had done to the lovely Makah people.

Yes, today, she would get the unpleasant duty over with, then concentrate on her own plans for the future. She hoped her future would include Proud Eagle.

But she knew that he had his people and their feelings about her to consider. She had only begun to prove to them that she was a kind, caring woman. After her father had gone so far in cheating them, it might take much more than her gestures of kindness to totally change their minds.

"My people call this fog-shrouded wedge of land the beginning of the world," Proud Eagle said, interrupting Billie's thoughts.

"It is lovelier than one could ever imagine," Billie murmured. "Seattle's forests have always enchanted me, but this is even more breathtaking."

She gazed at Proud Eagle from her seat in the middle of the canoe. He sat at the far end, rhythmically drawing his paddle through the water. He was dressed in only a breechclout today, his long, thick hair blowing in the breeze. The brightness of the sun made his beautiful face more copper and the uniqueness of his sculpted features and the intensity in his dark eyes more pronounced. She could hardly keep her eyes off his rippling muscles.

She didn't feel especially pretty today, for she had worn a casual skirt and blouse, which she thought might be appropriate for this sea venture. She wore slippers that could easily slip from her feet when it was time for her to enter the water, for they would need to leave the canoe to swim into the cave.

She noticed how Proud Eagle's paddle was ever so silent, its long, pointed tip keeping the water from dripping noisily. He paddled without even lifting the blade in the air while telling her that the canoe had been made from a single hollowed-out red cedar log, much smaller than those used by many warriors. The hollowed-out log was steamed by pouring in water and adding fire-heated rocks.

He had explained that when the sides were softened in this way, they could be flared, yet could keep the strength of straight-grained wood. Then the hardened gunwales were laced on to protect the hull from the constant wear of paddling.

Carved with a design of water creatures, and inlaid with bits of shells, the canoe had a vertical bow and stern with an elongated prow to break sea, or rough water. He was propelling the small craft with a five-foot ash paddle, paddling from a kneeling position.

Leaning against occasional rough water, he gained

equilibrium by throwing the craft to one side, leaning over the gunwale, and thrusting his paddle deep to catch and force water under the craft.

When he had told her that they were going to the cave today by canoe, instead of swimming there, she had been surprised since the cave entrance was not that far from shore.

He had said that he would explain after they arrived at the cave entrance. She was impatient to know, but did not press him to tell her.

The fresh sea air sent occasional soft sprays of water on Billie's face, and she would taste the salt on her lips.

It was invigorating. This was such a lovely place to be, especially since she was with the man she knew that she was falling in love with.

"It is so beautiful here," Billie said, gazing past Proud Eagle to the shore past the tall Norway pines, down the sandy beach and rocky cliffs.

He was navigating his canoe in the direction of where they swam only yesterday. It would be a place that would live forever in her memory.

"My people have lived here for generations," Proud Eagle said. "If the white man does not continue to take land from us, there will be many more generations of Makah to enjoy this land and sea."

"I'm sorry that the United States government tricked your people," Billie said quietly. "But it is not only the Makah. All men and women, as well as their children, who do not look white have been treated unjustly. It shames me to know the depth of deception that has been used to take the red man's land."

"When they took Makah land, they also denied us a part of the sea, for land that belongs to whites contains the shoreline from which the Makah fishermen launch their powerful whaling canoes," Proud Eagle said. "My White Owl Clan of Makah are not so much sea people, but they do need to fish to sustain themselves through the long winter months."

He knew she was excited about seeing the hair seals again today after having seen the babies yesterday. He would not tell her that those hair seals were one of the sea creatures that his people harvested for food. They were actually considered a delicacy.

But in time, when she was his wife, then she would have to know what foods she would be preparing for her husband. He had known that one day he would find the right woman who would take Soft Wing's place in his heart. He would never have thought that it would be a white woman, but there was no denying how quickly his heart had been taken by Billie and if she wanted it, it could be hers forever.

Even if it did seem so sudden, he knew without a doubt that she had become a part of his life for a purpose. Destiny had led her to him.

"My people call themselves Kwih-dich-chuh-ahtx, people who live by the rocks and seagulls," Proud Eagle said, wanting Billie to learn about him and his

153

people. He wanted to make certain that she was willing to become one with them and their ways before bringing her into his people's lives as his wife.

Billie started to say something, but her attention was diverted by movement beneath the water.

"That is a trout," Proud Eagle said. "See how the giant silver fish gleams in the clear prism of the sea?"

"Oh, and look over there!" Billie said, her eyes widening as she pointed. "They are so fascinating. I have seen them in the waters of Puget Sound, but never like this."

Several fur seals were asleep, floating on their backs in the water, their hand flippers curled onto their chests.

Proud Eagle was taking the canoe so quietly through the water it did not disturb the sleeping sea creatures.

Then Billie gasped when she saw more activity beneath the water. She could see cuttlefish flashing in colorful hues, glass shrimp prancing, sea snakes snaking, and green turtles frolicking.

Farther out at sea, several sperm whales were forming what looked like a wagon wheel, with their heads in the center and their tails out.

"What are those whales doing?" she asked, drawing Proud Eagle's attention to the strange behavior.

"I have seen this many times," Proud Eagle said. "It is how sperm whale families protect themselves during killer whale attacks."

"How smart!" Billie said, then gaped openly at the

humpback whale farther out at sea slapping the surface of the water with its tail, over and over again.

"The whale does this to stun swarms of krill below, making it easier to gulp up a meal," he explained. "In time, you will become as well acquainted with the activity at sea as I am. It is very interesting."

Billie realized how close they were now to the cave. The sea was still everywhere but around the cave's entrance; there it was thrashing madly. It was somewhat frightening, since she was going to swim into the cave with Proud Eagle. She wasn't sure now whether that was a wise thing to do. She was an excellent swimmer, but was she good enough to battle those waves and survive?

She looked questioningly at Proud Eagle, who also had noticed the rushing water.

"It will be safe enough," he said, reassuring her. "Trust me. I will make certain you are safe. But if you change your mind, I will understand. Most women are not courageous enough to do what you are about to do."

"They aren't?" Billie said, her throat suddenly dry. "Then perhaps I . . ."

"As I said, I promise to keep you safe, but if you would rather not do this, I would understand," Proud Eagle said just as Billie saw a baby hair seal being swept from the cave's entrance, and then another. They turned and swam back inside the cave, obviously unharmed.

But Billie couldn't keep her eyes off the furious water. The water at the entrance of the cave was so rough, it seemed as though some demon was hiding there, growling and fighting to be free of the water.

Now the canoe was as close as Proud Eagle was going to take it, and it did not seem strong enough to hold its own. She expected it to be dashed in the entrance of the cave at any moment, where it might split apart and be crushed.

Her heart pounded. She knew that Proud Eagle expected her to follow through on her promise to go with him. She didn't want to look like a scared jackrabbit. She wanted to impress him with her courage and stamina.

"It's so dark in the cave," Billie murmured, directing her fear elsewhere. "Might we get lost once we get inside?"

"I was wrong to suggest that you go with me into the cave," Proud Eagle said, realizing the foolishness of having asked this of her. He started paddling the canoe away from the cave, but stopped when she moved to her knees and placed her hand on the paddle to stop him.

"No, please," she said. Her heart beat like a thousand drums in her chest. "I'd like to see the babies. Please take me."

"Are you certain?" Proud Eagle asked, still holding his paddle steady.

"Yes, I am certain," Billie said, squaring her shoulders. "I'm a skilled swimmer. I can do it."

156

Proud Eagle started paddling again, for he realized that she felt she had to prove something to him. She wanted to show him that she could face anything.

He could see the rapid pulse in her neck, which showed she was truly afraid. But since she had said that she wanted to do this with him, he would not deter her.

He wanted her too much to pass up this chance.

Chapter Twenty-one

Proud Eagle took the canoe past the entrance until he came to where he could ease it between some boulders, so that it would not be carried away by the waves.

After securing it, he laid his paddle down and began twisting his long hair into a topknot. Next he reached inside a bag and took out several sticks.

"What are you doing?" Billie asked. She returned to her seat and held on tightly as the surf continued to challenge the strength of the small canoe, trying to dislodge it from its niche between the boulders.

"This is why we had to come by way of canoe today. These are spruce sticks," he explained as he inserted a few of the sticks into his knot of hair to hold it in place. "They will carry light with us into the cave."

"But how?" Billie asked.

He took a hinged shell that he had stowed beneath his seat and opened it, revealing a glowing coal.

One at a time, he lit the sticks like one would light a candle, then inserted the sticks in his hair.

"These will light our way," Proud Eagle said, smiling at her. "And they will momentarily blind the seals as we climb up the rocky perches inside the cave where we can observe them more closely."

"But won't the water put the fire out as you swim?" Billie asked, impressed by the Makah customs. She grew more and more spellbound by this man, moment to moment.

"I am skilled at this," Proud Eagle said with a grin. Then he grew serious again. "Remove your clothes. It will make it much easier for you to swim. That is why I wore only a breechclout today."

She hesitated for only a moment, then undressed down to her underthings. After all he had seen her in her wet, clinging clothes yesterday.

"Follow my lead and all will be well," Proud Eagle said, sliding over the side of the canoe into the water.

Billie again looked at the roiling water, still splashing angrily against the sides of the boulders that held the canoe in place, as well as in the cave entrance. Her heart pounded with fear, but she tried to think positive.

She marveled at how Proud Eagle could keep the fire on the sticks from being doused as he skillfully treaded water, waiting for her.

She smiled cautiously at him, then carefully slid over the side of the canoe into the water, which thankfully was not all that cold, but still so frenzied she had difficulty keeping her head above water.

"Follow me. We will be inside the cave very soon," Proud Eagle said. "Stay as close to me as you can."

"Believe me, I will," Billie said, now swimming alongside him as he moved closer and closer to the cave's entrance, making sure he did not leave her behind.

At this moment Billie was grateful that her father had taught her to swim in some of the most troubled waters of Puget Sound, ensuring that she would be able to swim herself out of any trouble she might find herself in.

Because of this training, she was able to keep up with Proud Eagle. Still, she was very relieved when they got inside the cave. The fire's glow lit things well enough around them.

Stopping to tread water beside Proud Eagle before choosing where they would climb onto the rocks, Billie became very aware of just how many seals were resting everywhere, on boulders and on the shelves of rocks at the sides of the cave.

As Proud Eagle had said, light from the burning sticks momentarily blinded the water mammals, long enough for Billie and Proud Eagle to climb onto a boulder.

Trying not to reveal just how cold she was, Billie sat stiffly beside Proud Eagle on the boulder. Thus far the seals hadn't been alarmed by their presence. Not that far away, one of them was stretched out on its side, making strange noises as two babies contentedly nursed.

The roar of the water as it came in huge waves into the cave was constant and deafening.

And after the seals' eyes adjusted to the light and the people, several of them leaped into the water and swam away, and one even left its baby on a boulder not far from where Billie sat.

"I wish I could hold it," Billie said. "Should I try?"

"If you wish," Proud Eagle said, as she crawled over to where the baby lay, its wide eyes glassy as the fire's glow shone in them.

Billie reached for the pup, but before she could get it the mother returned with a loud roar and a slap of a fin toward Billie. She quickly nudged the baby into the water, and both disappeared from the cave in one huge wave.

"I guess I should feel lucky that she didn't bite me," Billie said. She looked as far into the cave as the fire's glow lent its light. Tiny white cave crickets crawled along thin crevices. Occasionally a bat swept down into view, then disappeared again.

She sat down beside Proud Eagle again. She was trembling, and her skin looked slightly purple in the light from the sticks.

"You are cold," Proud Eagle said, reaching over and touching her shoulder.

His gaze swept over her scant clothes and took in the loveliness of her curves. He ached to run his hands over her body, not only to warm her flesh but to feel the wonders of her soft, white skin. The thought brought a sensual warmth to his loins.

"I am freezing," Billie said, her teeth chattering.

Proud Eagle put his arm around her shoulder and drew her closer to him, then with a finger, he lifted her chin.

He brought his lips to hers in a passionate kiss. She twined her arms around his neck and pressed her body against his. He could feel her exquisite breasts against his bare chest.

He slid a hand between them and kneaded a breast through her lacy garment. He could hear her catch her breath as he slipped his fingers up inside her clothing and filled his hand with its fullness, causing the nipple to harden against his palm.

Billie's whole body melted as his hand molded her breast—a sensation so new she could not think of anything that could feel as wonderful.

She wanted to experience everything with him that would bring out the woman in her. She had saved herself for the right man. And Proud Eagle was that man!

Proud Eagle put his hands on her waist and lifted her so that she sat on his lap facing him. He wrapped her legs around his waist, then hotly kissed her and thrust himself up against her, so that she felt the full outline and strength of him.

Billie clung to him and gasped as she felt what she knew was his manhood. The fabric of his breechclout and her underthings formed only a thin barrier that kept them apart in the way her body now ached for.

Never in her life had she felt such passion, such need!

At the sound of splashing in the water they drew apart.

Several of the larger seals were returning to the cave, grunting as they pulled themselves up on the rocks.

When one of them strayed close by in the water, its bulging eyes studying Billie and Proud Eagle, Proud Eagle took Billie by the hand and led her farther away, then helped her into the water.

They swam free of the cave and back to the canoe.

After they were safely there, Proud Eagle removed the sticks from his hair, then loosened it until it hung long and wet down his back.

He embraced Billie. "I have never wanted a woman as badly as I want you," he said huskily. He lowered his lips to hers.

He held her tightly as he kissed her, but her trembling caused him to hold her away from him and notice the color of her flesh. He knew that he had to get her to warmth quickly.

"Put on your clothes, and then wear this until we return to my village," Proud Eagle said, holding a sealskin cloak out toward her.

"But you are surely as cold," Billie said, as she accepted the cloak and put it around her shoulders, loving the warmth it was lending her.

"I am used to the cold," Proud Eagle said, as he shoved the canoe farther out into the water.

Billie sat down and watched as he knelt and silently propelled the canoe through the water. The warmth of the sun was a blessed thing, as she still trembled.

She realized, though, that a lot of the trembling came from somewhere else deep inside her. She knew that not long from now she would be making love for the first time in her life, for there was no doubt that after they returned to his longhouse they would finish what they had started in the cave.

"Are you warmed yet?" Proud Eagle asked, as he gazed at her.

"Enough," Billie murmured. Then she smiled. "Thank you for taking me into the cave. I shall never forget it."

"Nor I," Proud Eagle said, mainly referring to being with her.

He did not see how he could have ever looked at her in any other way than with adoration.

"I love you," Proud Eagle blurted out. His eyes searched hers. "I have never said that to any other woman besides my wife. I have never wanted to."

"I have never told any man that I loved him," Billie said, her voice quaking. "But I have fallen in love with you. It happened so quickly, yet it truly has happened."

"We shall find a way to make this work for both of us," Proud Eagle said firmly. "We were destined to meet. I have always believed in destiny."

"So have I," Billie answered.

The village was in sight a short distance away. Billie sat snuggled beneath the cloak as Proud Eagle took the canoe onward.

She could hardly wait to be alone with him . . .

Chapter Twenty-two

As Proud Eagle placed wood on the glowing embers of the fire in his fireplace, Billie anxiously awaited the warmth. Although the sun had been warm today, the air was cool.

After leaving the canoe, she had hurried with Proud Eagle to his lodge, clutching the sealskin cloak around her shoulders.

She had been very aware of how the Makah people stopped to stare at her, especially those who were busily tearing down the houses that had been too damaged by the mud slide ever to be used again.

She felt the resentment in those stares and avoided meeting their eyes.

"The fire will warm us soon," Proud Eagle said. He rose and turned to Billie. He smiled. "Your cheeks are pink now. That is good."

"I'm not trembling as much, either," Billie said, laughing softly.

She was just beginning to feel the awkwardness of the moment. Her belly took on a strange sort of warmth at its pit. It felt so pleasant she wished it would never go away.

"And so this is my home," Proud Eagle said, gesturing at their surroundings. "It is vastly different from yours. Does that matter?"

"How could you ask that?" Her eyes held his as he came to her and gently lifted the cloak from her shoulders. "I am with you. That is all that matters."

He framed her face between his hands. "My woman," he said huskily. "Are you . . . my woman?"

"I will be everything that you want me to be," Billie said softly. She stroked his cheek. "I can't believe that you feel this way about me. How can you forget. . . ?"

"Shh," Proud Eagle said, interrupting her. "You are not your father, nor anything like him. You are so much more than I ever thought I would even want in a woman. You are special, ah, so very, very special."

"As are you," Billie murmured as he drew her into his embrace.

She trembled against him as he lowered his mouth to hers and gave her a kiss that was so overwhelming, she moaned.

He slid his fingers up inside her skirt, stopping where her heart seemed centered. He began stroking her and Billie's knees almost buckled from the pleasure.

"I do not have beds such as you are familiar with," Proud Eagle whispered against Billie's lips as his fingers continued to stroke her.

It was as though she had grown wings and was floating in the heavens above herself, she was so light-headed from the throbbing passion that was enveloping her.

"I do not need a bed at all," Billie whispered back to him, her eyes closed, her heart pounding.

She gasped softly when a finger moved into the place that no hands had ever touched before. He began slowly thrusting, not going all that far inside her, but far enough to make her realize that she was coming alive to his nimble fingers in ways she would have never imagined. She felt a wonderful pulsing inside her that cried out for more.

He slowly removed his hand, then swept her fully into his arms and carried her from this outer room to another room that she assumed was his bedroom.

She vaguely saw through her hazed-over eyes the large mats on the floor.

They looked inviting and soft, yet even if they weren't, she wouldn't care. All she wanted was to feel the wonders of this man's body against her own. She wanted that part of her that ached now unmercifully to be fulfilled.

"The women of my village use cedar bark, cattail, and tule to make the mats used by my people for beds," Proud Eagle said, gently laying her on them. She felt the utter softness. "They are padded underneath with hides."

He reached for a pillow and placed it beneath Billie's head. "The women fill cedar bark pouches with cattail fluff for pillows," he said huskily, leaning down over her, his lips close.

"I care not what anything is made of," Billie murmured, smiling as she reached for him. "All I want is you."

He kissed her again and her hands stroked his muscled back, marveling at the softness of his copper skin.

She sucked in a wild breath of pure pleasure when he lifted her blouse and tossed it aside.

He leaned low over her and flicked his tongue across one of her nipples as he removed her skirt and other undergarment, rendering her nude for the first time before a man.

But all of this was a blur to her as his lips explored her body. He kissed her lips again, then stood over her and began lowering his breechclout slowly.

Billie could feel her cheeks flush as her excitement mounted.

Her blush deepened when he dropped his breechclout to the floor and she saw that part of a man's anatomy for the first time that she had heard about from married women.

And when he knelt over her again, his manhood touching her thigh, she felt its warmth.

"I shall be gentle," he whispered against her lips. "The first time for a woman can be uncomfortable."

"I know . . ." Billie said, causing him to lean back away from her, to look at her with surprise. "No. Please don't take what I've said wrong. I have never been with a man before, but . . . but . . . my women friends in Seattle explained to me how it was. I know that there is some pain when first making love, then there is much, much pleasure."

"It is good to know that I am the first," Proud Eagle said, then consumed her with a kiss as he began pressing inside her, slowly, gently.

And then Billie felt the pain. It was instant. And then as she had been told by her women friends, the passion began growing to something almost unreal, it was so beautifully wonderful.

She clung to his neck as he began his rhythmic strokes, his lips on a breast, his tongue flicking.

And then suddenly he held himself away from her.

He gently spread her legs and knelt over her.

She gasped as he touched her there with his tongue, flicking it over that part of her that suddenly seemed alive, it reacted so violently to what he was doing.

The pleasure was so intense, she groaned. Her head thrashed back and forth, then an explosion of stars shattered inside her head as that pleasure became twofold. She felt something akin to paradise.

Before Billie could catch her breath, he was inside her again, his lips on hers sending her into another world of wonder that overwhelmed anything she could have ever imagined.

Clinging breathlessly to him, she felt the pleasure beginning again, building, building . . .

Proud Eagle felt the fire raging within him, spread-

171

ing to a golden glow as he held her body against his. He moved one hand over a breast and down over her ribs until he was again at her moist channel.

He could feel her giving herself over to the wild ecstasy of sensual abandonment.

He was very aware of her gasps becoming long, soft whimpers.

He thrust into her, over and over again, until there was a great shuddering in his loins, flooded by passion.

He felt her straining up against him, crying out at her fulfillment as he found his own.

He thrust inside her for a moment longer, until he came down from that plateau of sheer ecstasy, then his body subsided, exhausted, into hers.

He still lay atop her, his arms enfolding her as her hands caressed his back, her lips gently nibbling on his neck.

Then Billie stroked his thick black hair, loving its smell, its feel, its sheen. She was reminded of her own hair and cursed herself yet again for having cut it. She wanted to look as feminine as she felt. She had never known love could be this wonderful, but there had never before been a man such as Proud Eagle. It amazed her still that she was there with him.

"Stay here. I must get something for you," Proud Eagle said, standing and gazing passionately down at her.

She did not feel the least bit self-conscious that he

was still as nude as she. It seemed natural that they would feel comfortable in this way.

She nodded and watched him leave the room, then snuggled down into the softness again. She closed her eyes and relived those past moments when she had discovered exactly how it felt to be a woman.

Her eyes opened as she heard him come into the room again.

She sat up and saw a wooden box in his hands, beautifully embellished with seashells. He sat down beside her, set the box between them, and opened it.

She looked puzzled. "It's a white cream," she said. "What's it for?"

"My woman, elk and deer tallow is used to make this cream," he said, slowly rubbing some on one of her cheeks and then the other. "It protects against chapping. Since we were in water, I felt this would be a good time to introduce you to the special cream."

"It feels wonderful." Billie sighed and closed her eyes as he gently rubbed it into her cheeks. The feeling was exquisite.

She shuddered sensually when he began applying it to one of her breasts, her nipple hardening at his touch.

"It is so soft . . . so . . ."

A slight whining outside the door caused Billie's eyes to open and Proud Eagle to draw away from her. He wiped his hands on a soft cloth, then stretched out beside Billie and reached for Snow as he romped into the room. The dog stretched out on his chest, his dark eyes gazing into Proud Eagle's, his tail wagging.

Billie ran her hands through Snow's soft, fluffy fur. "He is so beautiful," she said. "I can understand why Many Winds would want Snow with him at the boarding school."

"Many Winds has come to an understanding about it," Proud Eagle said.

They sat up, and Snow settled down in a tight ball of fur between them, content now that he was getting some attention.

"He misses Many Winds," Proud Eagle said, gently stroking the dog's curly locks. "But he is also learning that it is something that he must get used to. It is important for Many Winds to learn, in order to survive in a world that sometimes looks crazed."

"Yes, I know what you mean," Billie said as her thoughts went quickly to the lumberjacks. She wondered how they were going to react to her news. She dreaded it. But for now, she would savor these moments.

"The fleecy coats of our people's small dogs are removed and spun and used as warm blankets during the cold winter months," Proud Eagle told her. "Snow's fur will be removed next spring and used for blankets for the coming winter. By winter, it will have grown back in and will give him warmth during the cold days and nights."

"He is so pretty," Billie said. "I can just imagine how much Many Winds is missing him."

"All children miss their pets while they are in school, and all children are learning that lesson as well as everything else life hands them," Proud Eagle said.

"Everything about today has been wonderful," Billie said, reaching over and gently touching Proud Eagle's cheek. "But I can't stay much longer. I have things to do today that must be done."

"And they are?" Proud Eagle asked, taking her hand and kissing its palm.

"I will be telling the men that they must find employment elsewhere. It won't be an easy task. I dread it."

"But it is something good that you are doing for my people," Proud Eagle said. He drew Billie onto his lap and wrapped an arm around her waist. "In time all of my people will understand what you have done and will appreciate it."

"I want their respect," Billie said, swallowing hard. "I feel so bad about what Father did. I loved him, Proud Eagle, but as I said before, I never knew how cruel and calculating he could be, not until after he was gone."

She hung her head and wiped tears from her eyes. "I miss him, though," she said, her voice catching. "I miss my mother, too. I have no one left."

Proud Eagle lifted her chin with a finger. "You

175

have me," he told her. "You will soon be family, for I want you to marry me. Be my wife."

Tears filled Billie's eyes again as she gazed into his. "I want that so much. I want you so much."

"I am yours, forever and ever," Proud Eagle said. He drew her lips to his. "With this kiss I seal our future—our love."

He gave her a slow, soft kiss, then leaned away from her again. "When can you finalize things in your old life and enter your new one? I am anxious to have you with me."

"Soon. Very soon." She swallowed hard and smiled sweetly at him. "I am so glad you want me."

Again he kissed her, then questioned, "Are you certain about all of this?" he asked guardedly. "Are you certain about making such a big change in your life? Life here is vastly different from the sort you have always lived."

"I know, but I need no more time," Billie said. "Why? Are you . . . doubting my word . . . my feelings?"

"You know that this has happened quickly between us," Proud Eagle said, his voice somewhat drawn. "How can you be certain it will be everlasting for you? My life is so different from yours."

"You sound as though it is you who are having second thoughts," Billie said, stunned that he seemed hesitant now. "Are you?"

"No, I know deeply within my heart that I can never love anyone but you," Proud Eagle said. "But

I just want to be certain that what you feel can be everlasting. You have lived such a wealthy life. My home is small and without many comforts."

"You are all that I need," Billie said, brushing kisses across his muscled chest.

"Do not go home yet," Proud Eagle said, bringing her eyes quickly to his. "Stay. Stay the full night. Go with me tomorrow to see a stretch of land I have yet to harvest. Be with me a little while longer before going to break your news to the men. You might find that you will need more time to finalize things in your life before you can come and be a part of mine. I want these last hours with you before I have to wait for the rest of our lives to begin."

"All right," Billie answered. "I will stay."

Proud Eagle believed that Billie truly loved and wanted him, yet he worried that a tiny part of her who was the daughter of a rich lumber baron might find it too difficult, in the end, to leave it all behind.

Tomorrow, he would bring Billie to a new stretch of land that had not yet been touched by man. He meant to test her. Would she be tempted to take her lumberjacks there to harvest it after all? Or was she genuinely trustworthy and truly did not want that life?

"I can't wait to see the new land with you. I love seeing unharvested land. It is so lovely when it has been untouched by man," Billie said, her eyes twinkling with excitement.

"This land, every inch of it, has always been everything to us Makah," he said solemnly. "As it will be until the end of time. I just have to make certain that no more white people come and take what is ours!"

Billie went quiet, for she was feeling guilty again for what her father, Roy, and the lumberjacks had done to the Makah.

She would take on the chore herself of making certain it never happened again. She was there not only because she loved Proud Eagle but because she wanted to be sure he and his people were never cheated again.

"I'm hungry," Billie said, changing the subject.

"Wait here with Snow and I will see that food is brought to us," he said, hurrying into his breechclout. "It will not take long."

Billie smiled up at him, then hurried into her own clothes, which were now dry.

She picked Snow up and carried him to the outer room, then sat down before the fire.

As she stroked his thick fur, she felt a contentment that was new to her.

She smiled at the thought of how it would be for her for the rest of her life as she lived this dream with the man she loved.

Until she thought of Roy Clawson and the others. Roy's fate was already sealed. He should be gone by the time she arrived at the mansion tomorrow.

Was she really wise to wait another day before telling the others the news?

"I need this time," she whispered to herself, nodding.

She stared into the flames of the fire and got caught up in memories of her mother and father. The sort of life that she had lived with them would soon be behind her.

She was anxious to start the new life that she would have with Proud Eagle.

Surely nothing would stand in their way.

Chapter Twenty-three

It was so good to be riding alongside Proud Eagle in the brisk morning air as he took her exploring.

It had felt foreign to her to wake up beside him, instead of alone as she usually did. But as soon as he drew her into his arms and told her again how much he loved her, her world was all right again, and she knew that she was where she had been born to be.

She had loved sitting beside the fire and listening to him talk about himself and his customs, especially why the trees were so important to him and his people. They not only made money from what they shipped to Seattle, but the trees were used in many ways by the Makah.

She now knew that white cedar made neat and highly elastic bows, their backs covered with elk sinew. The same material was used for stringing the bows, laid on with glue made from sturgeon.

He showed her his own bow, a weapon two and a half feet long and two and a half feet wide at the center, tapering down to one half inch at the ends.

They made fishhooks and spears from bones.

Ash and cedar were used in making dishes, bowls, trays, and ladles.

And, of course, their homes were all made of cedar.

Now, as they rode farther and farther from the village, he told her about his people to help her adjust to living among them after she and Proud Eagle were married—which she hoped would be soon.

As soon as she returned home today, she planned to finalize things with the lumberjacks.

She hoped and prayed that Roy Clawson would already be gone. It would be wonderful if she never had to see him again. She couldn't understand how her father had tolerated him.

But when she thought about it hard enough, she knew that Roy and her father had had common bonds. They were both schemers who did everything for "self."

She was glad that she had her mother's personality. Otherwise she would not be able to live with herself.

"The forest is everything to my White Owl Clan, while the ocean is everything to other clans," Proud Eagle said, drawing Billie away from her thoughts. "My uncle, Brown Bear, and his Bluebird Clan, harvests whales, while my clan harvests lumber."

"But you do depend on some fishing so that you can have food to last throughout the winter," Billie said. She was glad that the sun came through a break in the trees just then, warming her face. It was hard to believe that she had swum only yesterday. Although it had been cold then, today it would have been impossible to get in the same water.

"Yes, and not only for food," Proud Eagle said. "My people manufacture an abundance of seal and fish oil. It is used domestically and commercially by steamships passing through the straits, as well as by some lumber companies that need such oils for their lumber mills."

"Yes, I know that my father purchased it indirectly in Seattle. He believed you would never sell it directly to him because of your differences," Billie answered.

"How do you know this?" Proud Eagle asked, giving her a quizzical look.

"I have been studying my father's business and private journals," Billie said. "I've read so much that has disappointed me in my father. But . . . that is in the past now."

"I can tell that your disappointment in your father lies heavy on your heart," Proud Eagle said tenderly. "I am sorry you had to discover the worst of how he was. It would have been best if you had never known."

"No, it is best that I do know," Billie said, swallowing hard. "Knowing makes me understand your feelings about him and what transpired between you. I am so sorry he interfered in the tranquility of your people's lives."

"We have learned from the past how to deal with

the present, and the future," Proud Eagle said. "Sometimes it was a hard lesson to learn, but once learned, it benefited my people in many ways that I cannot explain."

"I am just glad that you will not have to be concerned again about anyone causing mud slides, or interfering and cutting trees that belong to you," Billie said. "I will see to that myself. After today, the lumberjacks in my father's employ will be gone from Eagle Bay."

"Sometimes it is not that easy to rid one's life of such problems," Proud Eagle said. "So be wary, my woman, of what those men might do in retaliation."

"I am prepared," Billie said. "I'll be all right."

"Perhaps I should go with you when you tell them," Proud Eagle said, his eyes searching hers. "You can tell them, then leave and return to my village with me and stay there forever. We shall be married soon."

"I appreciate your concern for me and my welfare, but I have to do this by myself," Billie replied. "My father began this business alone, so I should end it alone. Once I get everything cleared up, I will come to you and never leave. Until then, please continue teaching me about your people . . . about the forest around us. It is so beautiful."

"I will gladly tell you what I know, but because your father was in the lumbering business, you probably already know that the red cedar is the most valuable of all trees that are cut in this area," Proud

Eagle said. A tiny twinge of suspicion about her prodding him to tell her about the trees sprang to life in his mind.

He felt guilty to have any doubts about her, yet she *was* her father's daughter.

"Yes, I do know that," Billie said.

"I have already told you that there are many things made from the trees that are used daily by my people," Proud Eagle said. "But there is much more to tell if you wish to hear."

"I want to know everything that I can so that I can prove to your people that I am worthy of being your woman," Billie answered. "And I want to please you."

"You already please me," Proud Eagle said, his eyes twinkling. "But if you wish to know, then I will tell you. Our lance heads? They are made of fool's huckleberry. Our gaming discs and children's bows are made from salmonberry, and float plugs are made from the redberry elder."

He gazed at her hair, still wishing that she hadn't cut it. "Our people's combs are made from salal and cascara and dogwood," he said, riding onward, Billie at his side on her own steed. "But again, the cedar is what is the most useful to us. Cedar splits easily and straight. It doesn't warp badly. Toxic substances within the wood resist rot and insect attacks. Its lightness, too, lets arrow shafts fly true and enables our canoes to be buoyant and paddle well."

"I saw how you looked at my hair moments ago," Billie said, reaching up and running her fingers through it. "It shouldn't take long to grow back. I, too, miss it."

"It is still the color of flame, and beautiful," Proud Eagle said, trying to make her feel better about what she had done.

"Mother's hair was the same color," Billie said, tears welling up in her eyes at the thought of her mother.

It just didn't seem possible that she could be gone. Billie could still hear her mother's soft laughter. She could still feel her gentle hands on Billie's cheeks.

Thinking of her mother brought Sara to mind.

Billie wanted to forget everything she knew about Sara and her father.

As outlandish as it was, Billie could now understand why her mother would want her husband to have a woman who could keep him happy in bed at night since she couldn't. She was that giving of a person.

So was Sara. Sara was good through and through.

Yes, she would in time be able to forgive Sara's role in this.

Proud Eagle reached over and brushed tears from Billie's eyes. "One day it will not hurt to think about those who have passed to the other side," he said. "Just know that they are in a better place and are content. When you think of your loved ones, they also are thinking of you and loving you."

"I would love to believe that," Billie said, as he drew his hand away. "Please tell me more about the trees and your people's use of them. It will help me get past this sad moment that I have put upon myself."

"Yew wood is dense and heavy," Proud Eagle said. "It is ideal for harpoon shafts and clubs. It serves well, also, for wedges. The western hemlock is stiff enough to hold shape well. And halibut hooks are hemlock made by thinning and smoothing a pencillike rod, then steaming and bending it in a kelp bulb set into fire-heated sand."

"I have seen that the Makah women are very involved in helping with many things," Billie said. "I am eager to discover my role in your people's daily life."

"In the summer, the women and girls walk the beach at low tide gathering clams, mussels, periwinkles, limpets, and sea urchins," Proud Eagle said. "They walk the woods and bogs picking salmonberries, huckleberries, and salal berries. The women gather from both the land and the sea. The forest and clearings, marshes and lake shores, serve as a garden and warehouse of plants. The Makah pick and dig and gather not only plant foods and medicine but also raw materials. Burden baskets are always used for the harvest."

"I have seen the women coming into the village with such baskets piled high," Billie said. "I hope to learn everything that will be expected of me."

"My women will share this knowledge gladly with you," Proud Eagle said. "For example, strips of

187

cherry bark are ideal for binding tool handles and sinew rope. The bark stretches when wet, shrinks when dry. Cattail fluff could be added to dog wool, then spun into yarn. There is much more, but I do not want to crowd your mind with anything else today. The women will be proud to show you."

Billie's attention was drawn to something overhead as it flew farther into the dense forest.

"Was that . . . ?" she said.

"Yes, it is a snowy owl," Proud Eagle said, having seen it himself. "My clan took its name from them. Long ago, many nested in our trees, then for a while they were gone. But now they are back, even more than before."

"Why now?" Billie asked, enchanted by the lovely bird.

"Shrews. A tiny animal that looks in many ways like a mouse," Proud Eagle said. "Both owls and eiders tend to nest in years when shrew populations are high, but not in years when they are low. The owls depend in large part on the shrews, but the eiders feed on aquatic insects and plants in ponds and streams."

"And the owls also depend on trees for nesting," Billie said. "If the trees disappear, so would that lovely owl."

"While the owl are on Makah land, they will never lack trees for their nesting places," Proud Eagle said, determination in his voice.

188

They rode onward, until Billie saw something that made her heart stop for a moment.

"I can't believe my eyes," Billie said, her voice breaking. "Father has trespassed again. This is your land, yet my father has roped some of it off. They are marked as Shaughnessy trees, although he had to know by treaty that it is your people's land."

"This is what I have had to deal with since your father's arrival in Makah land," Proud Eagle said tightly. "He daringly moved in, closer and closer."

"Well, neither he nor Roy will ever be able to do that again," Billie said, drawing a tight rein. She slid from the saddle, took a knife from her saddlebag, then marched over to the rope and sliced it in two.

She turned and looked up at Proud Eagle, who still sat in his saddle, straight-backed and somber.

"There. That takes care of that," Billie said. Her eyes wavered as they held Proud Eagle's. "I am so very, very sorry. As I said, I knew that Father had gone beyond what was his, but I had no idea he had gone this far."

"It has been a while since I have come to this part of our land. I had no idea your father had claimed it as his," Proud Eagle said, his voice drawn.

"I have just returned it to you," Billie said. She took the knife and slid it back in her saddlebag. "And I need to tell you of another place that I found while I was exploring."

Billie looked soberly at Proud Eagle. "I shall show

you when we are out riding again. I'm sorry, Proud Eagle. I did not know that my father was so eager for land that he would steal from you and your people."

She gave Proud Eagle another look of apology. "I believe I shouldn't go much farther today," she said softly. "I think it's time that I go and tell those men that their cutting days are over on Makah land. I don't want to wait any longer."

"I shall ride with you as far as you wish me to," Proud Eagle said, slapping his reins against his horse's rump as Billie slapped her own horse.

"I will ride with you to your village, then I would prefer to go the rest of the way alone," Billie said, her voice growing stronger, as was her courage. "Soon those men will be out of your life, as well as mine."

"I have dealt with Roy Clawson. I do not believe he will leave all that easily," Proud Eagle said. "My woman, be careful. Keep an eye on your back until you know that he is gone. I just cannot see that man taking orders from you."

A shiver raced up and down Billie's spine at the thought of what Roy might be capable of. "Yes, I know," she said. "And I will."

They rode onward until they arrived at the outskirts of the village. Proud Eagle sidled his horse over close to Billie's. He drew her lips to his and gave her a gentle kiss, then leaned away and gazed deeply into her eyes. "Again, be careful . . ."

Chapter Twenty-four

Billie was fighting off the fear she had of disclosing the news to the men, although surely they had already guessed what fate awaited them. Besides, Roy had probably told them the news. By having taken so long to tell them herself, she had given Roy time to work against her.

She left her house, her eyes focused on the bunkhouse. She could hear the buzz of conversation coming from the open door and windows, and then some laughter.

She also could hear the clink of coins, which meant that the men were idling away what was left of today by playing poker.

She shifted her eyes heavenward. The sun that had been so gloriously warm all day had sunk behind the distant hills. The sky had a few streaks of magenta left, but for the most part there was a darkening that made her task seem ominous and foreboding.

She regretted not allowing Proud Eagle to accompany her. Yet if he had, he would have been a part of the whole ugly equation, which might have resulted in harm not only to him but also to his people as a whole.

No. This was her job. She had it to do, and she was tired of putting it off.

With her jaw set and determination in her step she went to the bunkhouse.

When she entered, there was instant silence as all eyes turned to her. The men sat at a long table where the shine of coins was prominent, along with cards that each man held.

"Well, look what the dog dragged in," Roy spat out as he rose from his chair and walked slowly to Billie. "Now, what do you have on your mind this evening, Billie Boy? Or are you sure you want to tell us?"

He glared into her eyes. "Have you brought the gents glad tidings, Billie Boy?" Roy said through clenched teeth. "Well, spit it out. It's not like you to be wordless. Cat got your tongue?"

Even though she had expected it, Billie was no less unnerved by Roy's being there. He had obviously ignored her order to leave.

Billie knew that he was still there for only one reason—to cause her trouble!

She stiffened as she took a step closer so that they were only an arm's length from one another. "Step aside, Roy," she said between clenched teeth, his arrogance and threatening words giving her the energy and strength to complete her task.

She put a hand on his chest and gave him a slight shove.

"Why, you—" Roy snarled as he stepped away from her. "You'd better watch it—"

"Just shut up, Roy, and get out of my way. Go and stand with the rest of the men. I have come here for a purpose and I won't allow you to interfere," Billie said, her hands now on her hips as she stood before the men, who had risen from their chairs and were staring at her.

Roy grumbled to himself as he went and stood with the others, his hands in tight fists at his sides.

"I know how devoted you men were to my father, and I know that he would want me to thank you for it," Billie said. "I appreciate that devotion. And now that that is behind me, I have something else to tell you."

She paused and saw a sudden edginess among the men and a strange look in their eyes. She was certain that they already knew that they had lost their jobs.

She sighed heavily, then walked slowly around the table, eyeing them each, one by one. "I have come to tell you that I'm not going to sell out," she said, flinching when that brought looks of surprise into the men's eyes, and then sudden cheers and shouts. They looked as though the weight of the world had been lifted from their shoulders.

Billie went back toward the door, then stopped and faced the men again.

She slid a hand inside her skirt pocket and curled her fingers around her pearl-handled derringer. If any man was angry enough to challenge her with a firearm, she was ready to defend herself. She was well versed in the art of shooting guns. Her father had taught her as soon as she was old enough to hold this very derringer in her hand.

"No, I'm not selling out, but I am shutting down the business," she stated.

The men immediately grew angry, although no one said anything to her. The looks they were giving her alerted her that she might be in grave danger. Yet she stood her ground, ready should someone decide to take their anger out on her.

Her fingers were still gripping the pistol, ready.

"I'm sorry, men, but you have no choice but to find employment elsewhere," Billie then said. "I'm just not cut out to run this business. It's not something that I want to do."

"Your father would not want you to do this," one of the men said, visibly upset. "Please—don't do this."

"I have no choice," Billie said, swallowing hard. "There's more in life that I want to do than—than—felling trees."

The men turned to Roy. "Say something," a man shouted.

"You owned a good portion of the business. Surely you still have some say," another added.

"No, he doesn't have any say about this," Billie said tightly. "He gambled his portion of the business away. He has no say-so whatsoever about what happens to this business. And since I do, my word is final. Pack your bags. A steamer should arrive tomorrow morning. I would suggest you all be on it."

She turned to Roy. "That includes you," she said, her eyes narrowing angrily at him. "Do you hear, Roy? That includes you."

She felt an icy sensation race up and down her spine from the way he was glaring at her. It was a look that she had never seen before.

She turned on her heel and left the bunkhouse, stopping just outside to exhale. Then she hurried on to the mansion.

Truly afraid of what Roy might do, she locked all of the doors and windows, then went to the library and picked up a photo of her father and mother, their hands twined lovingly together.

"It's done," she whispered. "I only wish you could be happy for me, Father. I'm going to marry a wonderful man."

She smiled at her mother's face. "I know you'd be happy for me, Mother. He is such a wonderful man."

A loud cracking sound, and then a crash, made Billie drop the picture. The glass splintered and scattered all over the floor in glittering shards. She heard a rush of feet, and then a gun was thrust against her spine. She didn't have time to even grab her derringer. Suddenly she knew she had been right to fear Roy.

"Come with me," Roy growled.

"Where are you taking me?" Billie said, her voice breaking.

"Where no one can ever find you," Roy said, reaching around and sliding his hand into her pocket, quickly retrieving the derringer before she could stop him.

"You're wrong, Roy," Billie bravely said. "Proud Eagle will find me."

"No one will find you, not even that savage chief," Roy said, giving her a shove. "Now git. We've a ways to go."

"The men will see us leave," Billie said, walking out into the corridor. "Surely they don't approve of what you are doing."

"You've gotta be joking," Roy said, laughing throatily. "They know. I promised I'd take up where your father left off. No one'll ever know any different, not even your savage chief. He wouldn't know how to dispute my claim to this home and land.

"I'll just tell everyone that you chose not to stay here, but wanted to make a brand-new start elsewhere. If I need someone to back up my story, the men'll be glad to do the honors."

"Are you saying the lumberjacks are in on this?" Billie asked as he shoved her down the front steps.

She looked toward the bunkhouse and saw the men out on the porch, watching.

That was answer enough for her. They did know, and they were allowing it.

"I don't think I have to paint you a picture now, do I?" Roy said, laughing menacingly. "Now git to the stable. You're takin' a ride with ol' Roy."

"You won't get away with this" was all that Billie could say, fearing what he might do. There would be no way on earth that Proud Eagle could know what transpired here.

If Roy claimed that she had had a change of heart and had left for parts unknown, how could Proud Eagle prove otherwise?

"Your grieving over your father's death got to be too much for you, and you needed a new life elsewhere," Roy said. "That sounds good to me. It will to everyone else, too."

"You will pay for this one day," Billie said, her voice breaking. "Proud Eagle won't believe your story. He won't stop until he finds me."

Then her throat constricted when she thought of Sara. Where was Sara?

Chapter Twenty-five

Many Winds ran through the forest with Snow yapping happily at his heels. He realized the trouble he could be in and felt guilty for letting his father down again, but he had not been able to stay away from Snow. They were of one heart, one spirit!

Many Winds had had Snow as his constant companion since Snow had been born, the last pup of a litter of eight.

Snow had not been all that lucky. When he was born, he was so tiny that no one had expected him to live. The mother didn't have enough milk to feed Snow, so Many Winds had taken on the daily duty of feeding him a mixture of healthy herbs in milk until Snow finally proved to everyone that he was going to live.

The bond between Many Winds and Snow was so tight that it was all but impossible for Many Winds to go for too long without holding his dog and playing with him.

"Come on, Snow, keep up with me," Many Winds

called as he looked over his shoulder at his dog. He laughed. "Look at you and how you're panting even though it's a cold, crisp autumn day."

Many Winds had known that the temperatures had dropped drastically through the night. The bedroom had been cold. His breath had made moisture on the window, before he found the courage to raise it and leave.

He had dressed as warmly as possible, and he brought a blanket with him as well. Even now the blanket was snuggled around Many Winds' thin shoulders, the ends flapping, though part of it hung to the ground, sometimes threatening to trip him. He planned to go a bit farther.

He had left just before daybreak, when he knew his father got up and let Snow outside. His father was known to leave Snow outside for a while as he would go back to bed and get a few more winks of sleep.

That was what Many Winds had counted on today, that his father would leave Snow outside so that Many Winds could grab him and carry him quickly into the forest.

"I will be in trouble again, Snow," Many Winds said to Snow as the dog caught up with him and was running at his side again. "But you are worth it."

Snow gazed up at him with his dark eyes and barked.

"Shh," Many Winds said, looking quickly over his shoulder. "You bark too loudly. Its echo might carry back to the village and awaken everyone, especially Father."

He ran a while longer, then feeling as though he was far enough away to be able to play with Snow, he stopped and sat down on a log.

"Oh, Snow, I miss you so much when we are apart," he said as he whisked his pet up into his arms.

He laughed as Snow licked his face, then his laughter faded when he sensed something peculiar. When the wind blew and separated the yellow leaves of the trees for an instant, it gave Many Winds a view of a small log cabin.

He had been in this part of the forest many times, but he had never noticed the little building that sat amid the tall birch trees.

He could tell that it had been built only recently. The cedar logs were freshly cut, and the structure had been built in haste, for there was no mortar between the logs. It didn't even have a chimney or windows!

"What is it being used for?" Many Winds whispered as he set Snow on the ground.

Wrapping the blanket around his shoulders again, he crept toward the cabin.

He was beginning to get an eerie, foreboding feeling, as though evil spirits were lurking. He could not believe that this cabin had been built for a good purpose, and it was most certainly not built for someone to live in it.

It was on land that had been taken from the Makah

by treaty, but Many Winds felt as though it was all right to trespass on it.

"Come on, Snow, let's go and take a look inside," Many Winds said in a voice close to a whisper. "But please don't bark. You'll give us away should someone be close by."

Eager to investigate, Many Winds broke into a run, then slowed down and moved stealthily forward until he was at the door.

He saw a board that had been slipped across the door and secured, as though it was meant to keep something inside. He slid the board aside, then slowly opened the door.

Once his eyes adjusted, there was enough morning light for him to see into the interior.

Inside, the woman whom had been so kind to him lay curled up on the floor, asleep—or dead. Many Winds gasped and grew cold inside his heart. He didn't know what to do.

"Stay back, Snow," Many Winds cautioned as he slowly walked toward Billie. Up close, he could see that her wrists and ankles were tied together.

"You were brought here as someone's prisoner!" Many Winds gasped. "Who would do this? And why?"

He knelt and placed a hand on Billie's cheek gently, so glad that he could feel heat. She was still alive.

"Billie," he said, slightly shaking her by her shoulder. "Please wake up. Please!"

Through the haze, she heard the panic-stricken voice of someone she recognized. The child. Many Winds.

She slowly opened her eyes and found Many Winds kneeling down beside her. "Child! Oh, child, please help me," she said, her teeth chattering.

"I will, I will," Many Winds said, whisking his blanket from around his shoulders and wrapping it around her. "Can you walk? Or should I go and get my father?"

"No, I don't think I can walk," Billie said, her voice breaking. "But I'm afraid to be left here. He might return."

"Who?" Many Winds asked, trying to untie the ropes at her wrist, but not able to.

"Roy," Billie said, finding herself drifting again, so cold she felt numb.

"Many Winds!"

His father's voice shouting his name filled Many Winds with mixed emotions—fear that he had been caught disobeying his father again and relief that he was there to help the lady.

He knew that he could run away and hide, but he would not abandon this lady, no matter what punishment he would have to endure for his disobedience.

He rushed outside and shouted so that his father could hear, then sighed with relief when Proud Eagle ran into view, anger etched across his face.

"Father, please do not be angry," Many Winds said as he ran up to him. "I have been disobedient, but surely I was lured into it by the lady's spirit that beckoned me to save her."

"What lady?" Proud Eagle said.

He looked past Many Winds and saw the make-shift cabin.

"The woman with hair of flame. It's Billie," Many Winds rushed out. "Father, Roy Clawson brought her to the lodge and left her."

Afraid for Billie, Proud Eagle was scarcely aware of anything around him as he broke into a mad run toward the cabin.

He felt the blood rush from his face when he found Billie on the dirt floor, her eyes closed. She seemed scarcely to be breathing.

"I put the blanket over her," Many Winds said as he came and watched as his father swept Billie into his arms.

"That man is a dead man," Proud Eagle said as he carried Billie from the cabin.

"Father, what if the man is close by and sees what we are doing?" Many Winds asked as he followed his father, with Snow at his heels.

"He had better be far, far away from here, for he will not live to see another night!" Proud Eagle said, cradling Billie in his arms as he began running toward the village.

"I am sorry I disobeyed you again," Many Winds panted. "I will never do it again."

"We shall discuss this later," Proud Eagle said, looking over his shoulder at his son. "But this time there will not be any punishment. You were drawn here for a purpose. You found Billie. If any more time had elapsed, she might have died. Or Roy might have returned."

They ran on, Many Winds continuing to look over his shoulder, fearing that Roy might be near.

"Father, I am afraid," Many Winds cried.

"Never fear evil, even when you are staring it straight in its eyes," Proud Eagle said tightly. "Courage will gain you much more than fear, my son."

The village came into view a short distance away, the sun a beautiful orange glow along the horizon.

"Run fast, Many Winds, and alert our shaman that his services are needed," Proud Eagle said as he gazed down at Billie's pale face. "Quickly, Many Winds! Quickly!"

Many Winds nodded, and with Snow still dutifully at his heels, he ran into the village and toward Blue Cloud's longhouse.

An eagle swept down from the heavens, its eyes drawing Many Winds' eyes to it. In those eyes was a message of hope. Suddenly Many Winds knew that the pretty, kind woman was not going to die.

Chapter Twenty-six

Proud Eagle knelt beside Billie where she lay on a thick pallet of furs close to his fireplace.

Blue Cloud came and did all that he could to help her, yet she still slept soundly. Proud Eagle was afraid that Roy Clawson had done something besides tie her up and leave her in the small lodge. But Proud Eagle would not venture there. He would not think the worst.

At least she was no longer shivering, and her normal skin color had returned.

"Father, is she better?" Many Winds asked as he came to sit beside Proud Eagle, Snow beside him. Many Winds swept Snow onto his lap and stroked his curly locks. "Had I not found her . . ."

Then Many Winds hung his head. "I disobeyed you again," he said, swallowing hard. "I need to know if my punishment will be terribly bad."

Proud Eagle turned to Many Winds and lifted his hand to his son's small shoulder. "It should be bad, for, my son, what you did *was* bad," he said solemnly. "But I cannot overlook that had you not left the school, you would have not found my woman. Had she been in the cold much longer, she might not be breathing now. I may need to rethink the rules about the Makah children being so confined at that school for such long periods of time."

"But the white people made those rules," Many Winds said.

"The white people have broken many rules that have to do with us Makah, so now is the time for the Makah to break some ourselves," Proud Eagle said tightly. He gazed at Billie again. "Yes, I will see that changes are made. But first I must make certain that my woman becomes herself again. As it is now, she sleeps too deeply, and too long."

"What are you going to do about that mean man?" Many Winds asked.

Many Winds didn't understand how anyone could be so cruel as to leave a woman tied up in a place like that tiny cabin, especially without fire.

"As soon as I know Billie will get well, I will go into council and make plans," Proud Eagle said, his eyes narrowing angrily. "He intended for her to die. If not from the cold, he would have come later and killed her in some other way. She was a thorn in his side. He wanted the thorn plucked! He wanted it to die!"

"Proud Eagle?" Billie whispered, her eyes fluttering open. She gazed over at Many Winds. "Many Winds."

Proud Eagle and Many Winds both leaned closer. Many Winds' eyes were wide with excitement to see that Billie had awakened.

Proud Eagle's heart thumped like distant thunder inside his chest to see his woman's eyes gaze into his, and then he saw a smile creep across her beautiful lips.

Proud Eagle leaned down and swept Billie into his arms. "I was afraid . . ."

"I remember being so cold," Billie said, twining her arms around his neck.

Proud Eagle held her away from him as his eyes sought hers. "I will never allow anything like this to happen to you again. Never!"

"Where is Roy?" Billie asked, slowly releasing her arms from around his neck. "He should be in jail. He shouldn't be allowed to walk free ever again. I even believe he might have caused my father's death. Now that he's done this to me, I am almost certain of it."

"He will not be free to wreak havoc much longer," Proud Eagle said. "I wanted to be certain you were all right before I went after Roy and those who helped him."

"I am all right," Billie said. "Please go and find that bastard. But don't do anything that might bring trouble to your people. Take him to the authorities. Let white men handle the evil of a white man."

Then something else came to her mind "Sara!"

"Sara?" Proud Eagle said, raising an eyebrow.

"I am afraid he did something to Sara, too," Billie said, shakily moving to lean on an elbow. She looked desperately into Proud Eagle's eyes. "Just before Roy took me away, I thought of Sara. I didn't see her anywhere. Surely Roy harmed her to ensure her silence."

"I will assign someone to go and search for her," Proud Eagle said.

"I will go for a warm pot of soup for you," Many Winds said. Snow inched up close to Billie, lay next to her, and went to sleep again.

"Many Winds, wait. How can I ever thank you for what you did for me?" Billie asked, tears filling her eyes. "You and Snow. You saved me."

"Seeing you here, all right, is all that I need," Many Winds said, beaming. "Now you and Father can get married. I will have a mother!"

"He wants us to marry?" Billie said, reaching over and taking one of Proud Eagle's hands. "That truly touches my heart."

Then she stopped smiling again. "I had a dream while I was sleeping."

She sat up slowly, glad when Proud Eagle slipped a blanket quickly around her bare arms.

She only now realized that she was wearing some sort of soft doeskin gown.

"A dream?" Proud Eagle said, tenderly running his fingers through her hair. "What did you dream?"

"It's about the Makah children, especially Many Winds," Billie answered. "Many Winds doesn't like

210

going to the boarding school. I have a large house. It will be left empty, unless—why not change it into a school for the children, Proud Eagle? They could attend the school during the day, then go home and be with their families every evening."

"You would give up the house for the school?" Proud Eagle said, touched by her suggestion.

Then his expression changed. "Thank you, but it would not work," he said. "It is by treaty that the children attend the white man's boarding school."

"All the government really wants is that your children are educated," Billie said. "Yes, their main purpose is to control you and your children, but don't you see? I can hire a lawyer to argue that point. Schooling is important. So why should it matter where they get their education, just so they get one?"

"White men's lawyers speak with forked tongues," Proud Eagle argued. "No. It would not work."

"Yes, some lawyers are not truthful in their dealings, but I have a friend in Seattle who would speak on your behalf," Billie encouraged. "But I believe there won't be any argument against your children going to school at my house, as long as you agree to use the same teacher and headmistress. And Anna and the teacher could hardly refuse when they will be living in a mansion, with their own servants to wait on them hand and foot."

"Is this not blackmail?" Proud Eagle said. "To give those women a place in the mansion?"

"If it is, what's wrong with it, as long as your

211

children get to go to school during the day, and come home to their families each evening?" Billie reasoned.

"Yes," Proud Eagle said, framing Billie's face between his hands. "You are a woman of wonder."

"I am your woman," Billie said, then she sighed heavily. "I . . . I must lie down.

"Please send someone soon to find Sara," Billie said, closing her eyes. "I'm so tired. I . . . need . . . to rest."

"Sleep. I will return soon with news about Roy," Proud Eagle said. He placed a gentle kiss on her brow.

Billie opened her eyes again. "There's something I don't understand. Why did Roy feel that it was safe to leave me in that place? Didn't he know that one of your warriors could happen on it and find me?"

"He knew that we would not go on that land," Proud Eagle said. "It is the most bitter part of the treaty. That parcel of land was taken from my people. It is land close to our sacred burial ground."

"But why were there so many trees there?" Billie asked. "I did not see one stump among them."

"Your father never cut there, I believe because he felt our people's spirits," Proud Eagle said. "I told my people to stay away. Leave it to the spirits. Seems my son forgot, and thankfully so."

"Yes, thankfully," Billie whispered, drifting off into a soft, pleasant sleep.

Proud Eagle rushed outside and called his men together. He didn't take the time to hold a full council. He had to go now and find the evil man to make him pay for what he had done to Proud Eagle's woman.

He would bring Roy back to the village for the night, then take him to the trading post jail tomorrow at the break of dawn.

Roy dismounted, then stopped suddenly when he saw the door to the cabin standing open. "Damn her," he said, stomping toward it. "She escaped. But how?"

He had not expected anyone to find her. He knew that since the Makah lost this land by the rules set down in the treaty, they had never been seen there. They knew not to trespass.

He hurried inside, and cursed when he saw the cut ropes where they lay on the earthen floor.

Then he noticed the white fuzzy fur, and knew where it had come from. One of the Makah's dogs.

He recalled the chief's son having a white dog with such fur. "Damn that brat," he said. "He did this. He found her and set her free. Now all the Makah will be out for my blood!"

He ran from the cabin, and mounted his horse then rode hard toward the mansion. He had to get help from the men. They would help hold off the Makah.

Sweating, his heart pounding, he rode until he arrived at the house. When he saw no one in the bunkhouse and no horses in the corral, he knew that he had been duped.

The men had run out on him.

"Now what can I do?"

He hurried back to his horse and mounted it again. Breathing hard, he looked in all directions, wondering which was the safest route to take.

No matter where he went, the Makah would surely find him, and when they did, he doubted they would show him any mercy.

Chapter Twenty-seven

Billie awakened to the smell of food. Her stomach's growling in reaction to the aroma attested to how long it had been since she had eaten.

"I have brought nourishing clam chowder for you," Many Winds said, smiling down at Billie when her eyes opened. "My best friend's mother made it from clams she dug only yesterday. It is good. I could not help but eat a quick bowl myself, before bringing some to you."

"I'm certain it will be as delicious as it smells," Billie murmured, giving Proud Eagle a smile as he ladled out a bowl of chowder for her and sat down beside her.

"Are you strong enough to feed yourself?" he asked. In his eyes she saw a keen concern.

"Yes, I think so," she said. She felt shaky as she moved into a sitting position and took the warm bowl in one hand, a wooden spoon in her other.

She was becoming more aware of the differences in the way she would soon live from the way she always had. She was used to expensive silverware and china, but as Proud Eagle's wife, she would be using wooden eating utensils, as well as bowls and cups.

She could bring some of the lovely things from her father's house, but she didn't think that would be appropriate.

"While you slept I sent warriors to search for Roy Clawson, and I also sent someone to the mansion to see about the woman you worried about," Proud Eagle said. "We should receive news soon about Sara. I told my warriors to return as soon as possible to let me know whether or not they found her."

"Thank you so much," Billie said.

The chowder was warming her now, and she even felt invigorated enough to get out of bed, but she decided to wait a while longer just to be certain she was really well enough.

She only hoped that she didn't get pneumonia from the long period of time in that terribly cold cabin. Just thinking about Roy Clawson leaving her there like that made resentment boil within her. She had never despised anyone as much as she did that man.

The sound of horses arriving at the village drew Billie's eyes quickly to the door, then to Proud Eagle. "Could it be . . . ?" she said, stopping when he jumped to his feet and rushed to the door.

"Roy Clawson," he said. "The warriors found the evil man and have brought him here."

"Thank goodness," she said, setting her half-emptied bowl aside. "I thought he might have managed to leave Eagle Bay somehow. But what of the other lumberjacks?"

When Proud Eagle saw her determination to stand, he went to help her.

Many Winds wrapped a blanket up around her shoulders as she steadied herself before going on to the door with Proud Eagle.

"I must question Roy myself," Billie said. She turned to Proud Eagle. "What will you do with him now that you found him?"

"He will be locked away for the night," Proud Eagle answered in a voice filled with steel.

Billie searched his cold eyes.

"Soon you will see and understand," Proud Eagle said. He slid an arm around Billie's waist. "Come outside with me."

Many Winds put moccasins on Billie's feet.

"Thank you," Billie said, smiling at the sweetness of the child, a child whom she would raise as her own with Proud Eagle. She looked forward to it.

Realizing that she was still weak, Billie fought to walk steadily beside Proud Eagle until they came to Roy, who had been pulled off his horse and now stood beside it. He gazed in fear from Proud Eagle to Billie.

"And so what's to happen to me now?" Roy stammered, his eyes narrow slits. "Are you going to treat me as any savage would—by burning me at a stake?"

"You are the true savage," Billie said, stepping away from Proud Eagle so that she could speak directly into Roy's face. Two warriors came and stood beside him, each holding him by an arm. "You left me to freeze in that cabin. And what have you done with Sara? Is she suffering the same fate somewhere else? Where are the other men?"

"Sara?" Roy said, cocking an eyebrow. "I didn't do nothin' to Sara. I forgot about 'er. As for the men, they all chickened out on me. They hightailed it outta here. Don't ask me where."

"Then Sara is all right?" Billie murmured, a wave of relief rushing through her.

"As far as I know," Roy said, shrugging. "Like I said, I just wanted to rid my life of you. You are the only one that ruined everything for me."

"Well, I think it's time for your comeuppance, Roy," Billie said, smiling over her shoulder at Proud Eagle.

"What sort of comeuppance?" Roy said, paling visibly. He looked slowly around him as the Makah people came from their lodges and stood in a wide circle behind Proud Eagle and Billie.

"After you spend a full night at my village, you will be taken to the nearby trading post, where they have holding cells for evil whites like you," Proud Eagle said. He went to Billie's side and again placed a protective arm around her waist. "I will give you up to the white community to see that justice is done. The sheriff will come for you on the next steamer that comes to Eagle Bay from Seattle. Until then, you will be incarcerated at the trading post."

"And when the time comes, if need be, I will see you in court and make certain you are dealt with in the right way," Billie said. She swallowed hard. "Tell me, Roy. What role did you play in my father's death? I just can't get past believing you did something on that fateful day."

Roy snickered. "You dumb wench, do you think I'd confess to something like that? I've got enough to fight off, now that you've gone over to the side of the enemy. You're a traitor to all that your father ever believed in."

"You are the true traitor and you know it," Billie said, then felt light-headedness sweep through her. She leaned against Proud Eagle. "I've got to go back to your cabin and sit down."

But first she stared into Roy's eyes again. "I will see that you burn in hell for eternity. My father's fate was sealed the day he met you and brought you into his business. If not for you, I know he would still be in Seattle."

"And then you'd not have met lover boy here, would you?" Roy said, then laughed throatily. "Billie Boy and her savage lover. What a combination."

"Take him to the one longhouse that has not been demolished yet after the mud slide," Proud Eagle told his warriors. "You know which one I mean."

"You'd best treat me decently or you'll pay at the hands of the United States government," Roy said.

"No matter what I've done, you've got to treat me decently."

"Take him away," Proud Eagle said, waving a hand toward the longhouse that sat where the others had already been demolished. Mud clung to its sides and was piled thick on the roof. You couldn't see the windows, and the door was just barely visible, where mud had been dug away enough for the ones who had lived there to go inside and rescue what could be salvaged after their devastating loss.

Roy saw where he was being taken, and had to be dragged the rest of the way.

"No, don't take me there," he cried. "It's surely filled with mud."

"That's the general idea, isn't it, Proud Eagle?" Billie said as she walked slowly beside him, his arm still in place around her waist, keeping her steady.

"Did you not have to sleep on an earthen floor in the small cabin?" Proud Eagle asked, his eyes searching hers.

"Yes," Billie said, shuddering from the mere thought of her time there.

"Don't do this to me!" Roy screamed. "Take me to the trading post now! Do you hear? Now!"

"You have no power over anyone, so keep silent," Proud Eagle said, watching as Roy was taken inside the longhouse, then closed in, the door latched tightly behind him.

His screams, which soon turned to whimpers,

could be heard even after Proud Eagle helped Billie back into his longhouse.

Again she sat down on the blankets close to the fire, and Proud Eagle was ready to sit down beside her, but he heard more horses arriving.

He went and opened the door, then smiled down at Billie. "The woman you know as Sara is safe now. She is here. My warriors brought her here to ensure her safety."

"Sara!" Billie said, managing to get to her feet again.

She went outside just as Sara was helped from the horse. When she saw Billie, she ran to her and hugged her.

"When they told me you were safe, I had to come and see for myself," Sara cried, clinging to Billie. "I was so afraid that Roy might . . . might . . . have harmed you. Even though Proud Eagle's warriors told me that you were safe at their village, I had to make sure."

"Yes, I am safe, but had not Many Winds found me, I would probably not have survived," Billie answered.

"Sara, you can stay with us until Billie is ready to set things right at the mansion," Proud Eagle said, watching the two women smile at the suggestion as they broke apart.

"Will you?" Billie asked softly, reaching a hand out to Sara's beautiful face. "Sara, I've forgiven you."

"I'm glad you have," Sara said, walking beside Billie toward the longhouse. "And, yes, I will spend the night. Then I shall go and gather my things and take the next steamer to Seattle. My time here at Eagle Bay is finished."

"No, I don't think so," Billie said, her eyes gleaming as they went into the lodge.

Billie sat down on the blankets and patted the pallet, urging Sara to sit beside her.

"What do you mean?" Sara asked.

"I have a wonderful idea," Billie said. She took Sara's hands in hers and told her about changing the mansion to a school for the Indian children.

"And you would stay on and continue with your duties as usual," Billie said excitedly. "Except it will be to the children and a couple of older women. The teacher and headmistress will be living at the mansion. That is, if they and the government agree to what I offer them. Sara, remember how you so badly wanted to be a teacher? Well, now is your chance to help at a school."

"It's a wonderful idea," Sara said, her eyes widening. "Oh, yes! Thank you, Billie. Thank you!"

"Yes, and I can hardly wait to go to school there instead of at the boarding school," Many Winds said, his eyes dancing.

Billie motioned to Many Winds. He went to her.

"Sara, meet Many Winds," she said, introducing him. "He will be one of the children at the school— and he will soon be my son."

"Son?" Sara gasped, looking wide-eyed at Billie.

"Yes, Proud Eagle and I are going to be married," Billie said, smiling over her shoulder at Proud Eagle, who still stood behind her, listening and watching.

"Married?" Sara gasped again. "How did this happen? When?"

Billie explained how it had all happened, delighting Sara with the tale.

"It's like something I would read in a romantic novel," Sara said, smiling. "It is so wonderful, Billie. So wonderful!"

"Yes, yes," Billie said, glad when Proud Eagle came and sat beside her, and Many Winds positioned himself closely in front of them, in his eyes a contentment that Billie loved seeing.

Snow came to Many Winds, settled onto his lap, and soon fell asleep.

"And this is Snow," Billie said, stroking the dog's fur. "I'll explain to you soon about how the dogs at the village give their fur for use in clothes and many other things."

"You already know so much about the Makah, don't you?" Sara murmured, looking slowly around the longhouse. "They live so differently from the way you have always lived."

"Yes, and I look forward to learning everything I'll need to know," Billie said, then felt overcome by exhaustion. "But now I need to rest again."

"Sara, I will take you to my widow aunt's longhouse, where she will gladly make up a bed for you tonight," Proud Eagle said, rising. He reached a hand out for her. "Come."

Billie saw Sara's hesitation. "Go on," she urged. "You will have a nice evening with his aunt. Everyone here is so kind and giving."

"On our way to the trading post tomorrow, we will see you safely to the mansion," Proud Eagle said. "I will leave a warrior to keep watch in case any of the lumberjacks decide to come back and make trouble."

"Thank you," Sara said.

She gave Billie a hug, then waited to leave with Proud Eagle.

"Proud Eagle, I want to accompany you to the trading post," Billie said, determined to go and see that Roy was actually placed behind bars.

"Will you be strong enough?"

"Yes, I'm most certain of it."

"Then, of course, you can go."

"I look forward to seeing Roy behind bars," Billie said, then snuggled down onto the blankets. "I must sleep a while now, though. I want to be ready to ride tomorrow."

Proud Eagle bent low and brushed a kiss across her lips, then left the longhouse with Sara.

Chapter Twenty-eight

The day was cloudy. It would be one of those dull gray days, when rain fell constantly from the sky, enough to ruin all activity outside of one's home.

Billie was just glad to be on a horse again and well enough to ride.

She glanced heavenward. She hoped that the rain would hold off until she got back to the village with Proud Eagle. He had persuaded her to stay one more night before returning to the mansion, to finalize things there before moving in with him.

She hoped the rain would pass by. There was to be a salmon bake tonight, as part of a celebration of life for the Makah. They had survived the latest incident, which could have been a horrid tragedy—the mud slide. And she and Proud Eagle would celebrate her safe return after being kidnapped.

She had much to look forward to. But there were two unpleasant things that had to be done before she entered into her anticipated life with Proud Eagle.

She must see to it that Roy Clawson was locked

behind bars at the trading post, until the sheriff from Seattle could come for him.

And she didn't look forward to going through her father's things, though she had to do that in order to ready the mansion for the school for the Makah children. Sara was at the mansion doing her part in getting it ready.

She could not see any reason why the government wouldn't agree to her proposal. The mansion and its grounds were a much better environment, not only for the teacher and headmistress but especially the children.

After Anna had thought about it, she would surely see that she and Freda would get much more cooperation from the children if they were able to return home evenings to be with their families. And Billie would not take no for an answer when she faced Anna with the plans, though Anna did have the authority to do as she pleased.

It was true that the children needed an education in order to stand up against the white community when they grew into adults. As it was now, some children resented being taken away from their families so much that they refused to learn. If they could be with their families in the evenings, they would surely take their daytime activities much more seriously and, hopefully, even eagerly.

But before anything else could occur, Billie would take a side trip to the school and tell Anna the plan.

"You will regret the day you left Seattle," Roy

growled from where he sat on his horse a few feet from Billie. His voice took her from her thoughts to him.

She shivered when she saw the intense hate in his dull eyes. The way he was glowering at her made her insides tighten. She knew that if he ever had the chance, he would finish what he had started in that tiny cabin.

But she didn't see how that could ever be a possibility. Once he was behind bars, that would settle *his* fate, not hers. A judge would soon hand down a ruling that would end Roy's evil ways forever.

"If Father could have seen the evil in your heart, he would have rid his life of you long ago," Billie said, her eyes narrowed in anger. "But he didn't, and he paid dearly for his ignorance. Roy, I know you had a role in my father's death. What did you do? How long had you planned it?"

"He was a fool," Roy muttered, finding it hard to sit in the saddle with his hands tied behind him.

He had to catch himself when he started slipping. If not for a rope tied around his waist and to the pommel as well, he would have fallen from the saddle altogether.

Billie saw him struggling and knew she would enjoy cutting the rope that held him secure. She was just glad that once he was left behind at the trading post, she could forget him—at least until she had to attend his trial.

Ah, yes, finally her life could truly begin. And

what a life it would be. She would be married to the most wonderful man in the world.

"A fool you call my father, yet he took you in and helped you become almost as wealthy as him," Billie spat. "*You* are the fool. You gambled your wealth away, then started planning how you could get Father's portion. How did you do it, Roy?"

"That's for me to know and you never to find out," Roy said, laughing. "But, if you need to know, yes, it was my plan to take over everything once your father was gone. I should've just burned the journals. That would've taken care of it. But I took my chances and you came out the winner. That's just my luck. Just like playing poker, I just can't seem to ever come out on top."

She stared at Roy, trying to see what her father had seen in him—the man that he trusted so much he didn't realize Roy was planning his demise.

Her father had helped the man get out of poverty and made him wealthy in his own right, only to have the man deviously plan to kill him. If only her father had not been too preoccupied with his business to notice. He would probably still be alive today.

"I realize that I may never know the truth, but you know this, Roy, I will absolutely make certain you can't swindle or kill anyone else," Billie said, then sank her heels into the flanks of her horse and rode away.

Proud Eagle had ridden up in time to hear the

exchange between Billie and Roy. He gave Roy a heated stare, then rode after Billie.

When he caught up with her, he saw her tears and wished that there was something he could say to take her pain away. Knowing who had taken her father from her had to cut like a knife into her heart. Yes, her father was a greedy, cold, and calculating man, but he was still her father.

"He is such a bastard," Billie blurted out as she gazed over at Proud Eagle. "He deserves what lies ahead of him."

"Today could be the last day you would ever have to look on his face again," Proud Eagle said. "There is enough proof of his evil ways without you being so involved in his trial. Why not concentrate only on us now? Leave the rest to the white man's authorities?"

"I just can't," Billie said, swallowing hard. "I want to bring out in court what he did to me. Although there is no absolute proof of what he did to my father, I can tell the judge what Roy just told me. And I will take the journals into court. I'll use them as proof."

"Then you do what you feel you must do," Proud Eagle said, nodding. "I will accompany you there. I will be there for you."

"Thank you," Billie said. She wiped tears from her eyes with the back of a gloved hand. "You are such a blessing. If not for you, I would be so alone."

"You will never be alone again," Proud Eagle said, then realized they were almost at the trading post. "Soon the man will be behind bars. Then we can go back to my village. The salmon bake is filled with much fun for our children. There will be much celebration. You are a part of that celebration."

"Our love for one another is cause for celebration," Billie said, smiling at him.

Then she gazed at the large cabin they were approaching that sat up away from the sea, yet close enough so that the large steamers could land at the bay.

She knew that fish, sealskins, baskets, and other items were shipped from this trading post to Seattle and other small communities along Puget Sound, whereas the steamers brought flour, sugar, and other desirable goods that were used by the Makah people.

Proud Eagle had told her that during the summer season, the work group was divided at Eagle Bay. Half worked with lumber, the other at sea. His fishermen had been known to catch and ship ten thousand pounds of halibut in one day on the mail steamer that came from Seattle three times a week to Eagle Bay.

With the fishermen bringing in thousands of pounds of halibut a day, women were kept busy cleaning and preparing fish for drying. The entrails were removed and left on the beach for the tide to reclaim just as the bones were later returned to the sea.

She had learned that the skin of the fish was wiped clean with ferns and that the flesh was cut into strips with the skin left on and hung over racks to dry in the sun.

Halibut was a mainstay for the Makah, available year-round.

The trading post was only half a mile from the village. When the next steamer arrived, word would be sent back on it to the sheriff at Seattle that a prisoner awaited him at the trading post.

Billie wasn't comfortable with the amount of time it might take to get Roy to Seattle, but she had to trust that the holding place for criminals at the trading post was adequate enough to keep him locked up until he could be taken elsewhere.

"You'll be sorry, Billie Boy," Roy shouted at Billie as they stopped at the trading post hitching rail. "I'll get you. You can't hide! Just you wait and see. I'll find a way to get you and kill you."

Proud Eagle dismounted, and went and cut the rope that held Roy on the horse, then gave the man a shove that caused him to topple over the side of the steed, landing him hard on the ground with a thud.

"You sonofabitch," Roy growled as he glared up at Proud Eagle.

Proud Eagle placed his foot on Roy's stomach and pressed down on it. "Every word that comes from your mouth is filth," he said with disgust. "You only dig your grave deeper with each word that is breathed across your lips. I advise you to be silent,

Cassie Edwards

ugly man. Do not speak again to my woman. If you do, I might change my mind and not wait for the white man to come for you. I will decide, myself, what your fate will be, and I promise it will not be quick. It will be painful and slow."

Roy breathed hard, his eyes bulging as he tried to roll away from Proud Eagle's foot, but he was unable to budge. "Just get away from me," he said between clenched teeth. "I . . . won't . . . say anything else. Please . . ."

"Now you ask for mercy?" Proud Eagle said, disgusted.

"Well, hello, Proud Eagle," Johnny Two Wings said as he stepped to the door of the trading post. "What have you brought me today?" He looked down at Roy, then smiled up at Proud Eagle. "I believe I smell a skunk."

"He is worse than a skunk," Proud Eagle said, stepping away from Roy. "Cousin, I have brought you the worst of men. Keep him locked up until the Seattle sheriff can come for him."

Proud Eagle went to his cousin, a half-breed, and gave him a hug. "It is good to see you, but this time I do not come for trading."

Proud Eagle explained to Johnny Two Wings why he had brought Roy for incarceration, then turned to Billie and reached a hand out for her. "And, cousin, I would like to invite you to a wedding."

"A wedding?" Johnny Two Wings said, gazing at

Billie. His eyes shifted quickly to her hair, his eyebrows lifting when he saw how short and red it was. "And this will be the bride?"

"Yes," Proud Eagle said, sweeping his arm around Billie as she came to his side. He made proper introductions, explaining who her father was, then glared at Roy. "I hope you do not mind taking this filth off our hands."

"It would be my pleasure," Johnny Two Wings said.

He reached down and pulled Roy up from the ground by an arm. "This man has made trouble for me more than once here at my trading post. He is not honest in his dealings."

"He is a coldhearted murderer," Billie said. "He killed my father."

Johnny Two Wings gave Roy a shove into the trading post. Billie and Proud Eagle followed them.

"I did not know your father, though I recognized him when I traded with him. Your father was a man of mystery to me. I never knew which mood he would be in."

Billie was uncomfortable. She could tell that this was another man who held no kind thoughts of her father, and surely had no respect for him.

It saddened her that the man she knew as a little girl had turned into someone she hadn't ever known.

"Cousin, if you did not have the responsibility of guarding the criminal tonight, I would invite you to attend our people's salmon bake," Proud Eagle said as Roy was taken to a cell. "But this is a tricky prisoner. I would not suggest leaving him alone."

"Don't worry, I reside at the back of the trading post, so he will never be alone," Johnny Two Wings said. He slammed the cell door shut with a bang, then turned the key in the lock.

Billie watched Johnny Two Wings carry the key and hang it on a nail behind his desk. Concern gnawed at her. But surely she was worrying for naught. Johnny Two Wings seemed very capable of taking care of things.

She gazed at him at length. She could see the half-breed in him. His coloring was more white than copper, and he had light brown hair. But his features were as sculpted as Proud Eagle's, and his eyes were as dark and as intense.

He wore buckskins, and his hair hung down his back in one long braid to his waist. He was pleasant, his smile warm and friendly.

"Do you need any supplies while you are here?" Johnny Two Wings asked, motioning toward the shelves stocked high with wares.

"No," Proud Eagle said. "I am anxious to get back to my village. I would like for Billie to see how things are prepared for the salmon bake."

"I am eager to learn," Billie said, smiling.

They walked outside and mounted their horses.

Proud Eagle gestured toward the mare that had

brought Roy to the trading post. "Take my mare as payment for your trouble."

"Your horses are the best I have ever known," Johnny Two Wings said, running his hands across the horse's withers. "Thanks, cousin, but you know it is not necessary."

"The horse is yours," Proud Eagle said, nodding at Johnny Two Wings. "Again, thank you for taking the filth off my hands."

"I will make certain he is kept locked away until the sheriff arrives," Johnny Two Wings said, leading the horse to the side of the trading post and putting it in his corral with his own. "Thank you for the steed, cousin, and it was a pleasure meeting you, Billie. I hope to attend your wedding."

"I will look forward to seeing you there," Billie said, giving him a short wave of good-bye.

After they were amid the trees, where golden leaves fluttered above them, Billie heard Roy shouting at her from the open-barred window of the cell.

"You ain't heard the last from me, Billie Boy!" he shouted. "Nothin' can keep me locked away. Nothin'!"

Proud Eagle and Billie exchanged quick looks.

"You have nothing to fear from him," Proud Eagle encouraged. "Those are only words."

"Something tells me that he will find a way to follow through on his threat," Billie said, visibly shivering. "He is such a snake."

"Your imagination is running wild," Proud Eagle said. He sidled his horse over closer to hers. "Relax, my woman. You have much merriment ahead of you. Tonight you will enjoy the salmon bake with my people. And then . . ."

Billie grinned, her eyes twinkling. "Then what, Proud Eagle?"

"You know," he said, chuckling.

"Yes, I believe I do," Billie said, feeling a warmth spread from the pit of her belly.

She anticipated that much more than a mere salmon bake!

Chapter Twenty-nine

The moon was big and full. The tide was high and splashing onto the beach in large curls, yet the breeze was gentle and sweet. A huge fire leaped high in the center of the Makah village.

Much laughter and the aroma of food filled the night air as everyone sat around the fire on comfortable mats. They were celebrating the huge salmon catch, as well as their new life free of interferences from the white lumber baron and Roy Clawson.

Tonight it was just the Makah looking forward to the wonderful promise of tomorrow.

Billie sat with Proud Eagle at her right side, her eyes sliding over to Anna, who sat on her left. The headmistress had joined the fun tonight. And all of the children were there also, since permission had been given by Anna.

Anna had quickly sent notice to the government about the plans for the mansion to be used as the school. The idea appealed to her selfish side, for it would be more comfortable for her and the teacher.

But she saw the huge house as an opportunity to add to the children's studies. More rooms meant more space to divide the students by age and education level.

Anna was proving to be a woman with a big heart. She seemed to understand the importance of the Makah children being raised in the Makah tradition.

"It is such a wonderful thing," Anna said, as she scooted closer to Billie. She nodded a thank-you to a woman who handed her a napkin made out of pounded cedar bark. "Just look at the children tonight. They are beaming."

"A lot of it is because of you," Billie said, smiling at Anna and taking a napkin herself. "Had you not spoken on behalf of the children attending school at the mansion and being able to return home in the evenings to be with their families, instead of being forced to live at the boarding school, you would not see those smiling faces tonight."

"No, and they would be feeling sad because they wouldn't have been allowed to attend the salmon bake," Anna said. "I'm starting to see that it was wrong not to allow them to join in on these traditional celebrations of their people. It was cruel of the government to mandate that they be kept from home as much as they were. I saw it in the children's faces every day, the sadness, the loneliness."

She reached over and took one of Billie's hands. "It's because of you, sweetie," she said, her eyes misting with tears. "You are the one who opened my eyes to so many things."

"Mine were opened first," Billie said. "I had no idea what my father was doing to these wonderful people with his lumber company, and I had no idea there were schools such as yours, where children were forced to live. When I saw the school and realized why it was there, I was shocked."

"It was meant to be something good," Anna said. She eased her hand from Billie's. "I just couldn't see past what I thought was best for them. Not until you came along and awakened me to it."

Anna chuckled. "Of course anyone who sees me at the mansion will believe I wanted the school established there because I will have such a beautiful room all to myself, and maids and servants at my beck and call," she said. "And . . . perhaps just a tiny bit of that is true, but the real reason is that the children will be better off."

"I wish Freda could have joined us tonight," Billie said, looking in the direction of the school.

"She's a wonderful teacher, but she's a bit timid, that one," Anna said. "But mark my word, she is as excited as the children to be able to have such a wonderful place at her disposal. She loves the children and wants only what is best for them."

"As we all do," Billie said. Many Winds suddenly appeared and knelt before her. Snow was panting hard from running along the beach with Many

Winds and his friends, as they played in the effervescence of the high tide.

"Come and run barefoot in the foam with me," Many Winds said, reaching for Billie. "It is such fun!"

"I promise I will when the next high tide rolls in," Billie said, not hearing Proud Eagle chuckle beside her. He knew that during the next full moon the winds would be too cold for anyone to run barefoot in the surf.

"All right," Many Winds said, standing and pulling Snow into his arms. "I am too tired, anyway. And my belly is grumbling. I am ready for some salmon!"

"Come," Proud Eagle said, patting the thick mat at his right side. "Sit beside your father. It is almost time for the plates to be passed around to everyone."

"It all smells so good," Many Winds said as he plopped down beside Proud Eagle. He held Snow on his lap. "Doesn't it, Snow? Are you hungry for salmon?"

Snow gazed at him with his wide, dark eyes and barked as though he knew what Many Winds had said.

Billie felt such a peaceful calm tonight, a wonderful warmth that being with Proud Eagle and his people gave to her. Tonight was the beginning of a new life for these people.

Starting tomorrow they would not have to wonder

where Roy and the lumberjacks would be cutting, whether or not it was on land stolen from the Makah!

Everything was theirs again, and Billie was there to make certain the United States government never cheated them again. She could read the fine print on the treaty papers. She knew exactly what belonged to the Makah.

She glanced over at Proud Eagle. He was such a proud man. He was such a wonderful leader of his people. He deserved nothing but the best, as did they.

And she looked forward to being a part of their lives.

She was so in love, she melted inside every time she looked at him. Just for him to touch her made her world a paradise.

She turned to her left and smiled at Anna as she handed Billie a pile of wooden plates, after taking one herself.

"I was told to pass these along to everyone else," Anna explained.

"Thank you," Billie said. She slid one off for herself, then passed the stack to Proud Eagle.

Soon after, large platters and bowls of food came down the line, each person taking a portion, then passing everything on to the next.

A good assortment of food was on Billie's plate, all of which smelled tantalizing. She had taken a little from each dish that was offered, most of which she did not recognize.

She smiled at Proud Eagle.

"I understand that you are unfamiliar with my people's foods," he said, grinning at her. He began pointing out individual foods to her. "There you have seagull eggs, dogfish shark livers, and eelgrass stalks. You have also taken some salmonberry and thimbleberry sprouts. There you have dried and toasted fish fins and gills. And then the last thing you took is our prized salmon."

Billie scarcely heard him say "salmon," for her eyes were still on things that looked anything but appetizing to her.

Eelgrass stalks? And toasted fish fins and gills?

She hoped Proud Eagle didn't see her shudder.

"I see that you do not like the sound of some of the food," Proud Eagle said, chuckling.

"Dogfish shark livers?" Billie said, visibly shuddering. "And . . . and dried and toasted fish fins and gills?"

"In time you will find them to be a delicacy," he said, popping a toasted fin into his mouth.

Billie watched him chew it and saw that it didn't seem to have an adverse affect on him. Instead he actually enjoyed it.

She bravely took one herself and ate it. It tasted like deep-fried wild mushrooms.

She chanced a bite of the dogfish shark livers and enjoyed them as well. They were no different than the livers and onions that her mother had prepared at least once a week when the entire family was at home. It brought wonderful memories of family life back to her.

"Of course, the salmon is the most delicious," Proud Eagle said, plucking a piece of salmon. He smiled as he chewed it, savoring its taste.

"I have always liked salmon," Billie said, before taking her own bite.

"Salmon are netted in late summer and fall as they are headed to spawning grounds," Proud Eagle softly explained. "They swim through salt water to start their freshwater runs in the rivers and streams. They are caught by hooking, harpooning, or shooting with arrows. In some places, latticework weir nets act as obstructions, concentrating the fish and making them easier to catch."

Billie took another bite of salmon. She preferred it over everything else she had on her plate, although she was determined to eat everything before she was finished. She wanted to show that she was able to overcome any obstacle that she was faced with in order to be a good wife for the Makah chief.

"It is a long winter," Proud Eagle said. "Fish are steamed and dried and stored for those long sieges of cold weather. My people are experts at food preparation that permits storage. Air-drying and smoke let my people draw year-round on the seasonal abundance brought in from the sea. But a lot of the salmon my warriors catch are shipped off to the canneries in Seattle. Those canneries prefer sockeye salmon. It has been a good sockeye year."

"I think it's interesting how the salmon was prepared for tonight's salmon bake," Billie said. She noticed that Anna had not hesitated at eating anything. She was truly enjoying the feast and the merriment of the people that went along with it. Billie was glad that she had invited her there. The closer they could get in a friendship, the better it would be for the children.

Proud Eagle looked over to where the salmon had been prepared for tonight's feast. "They are steamed in a wrap of salal leaves on hot rocks set into a pit and covered with fern fronds."

"Next year I want to help prepare them for steaming," Billie said. "I want to make you proud."

"You already make me proud," Proud Eagle said, taking her empty plate and setting it with his on the ground. "Come. The tide is receding. Let us watch its retreat alone, while everyone continues to enjoy their evening beside the fire."

Billie smiled at Anna, then left the feast behind as she walked hand in hand with Proud Eagle, still finding it hard to believe that she wasn't dreaming all of this. Not long ago, she had lived so differently. Now she wanted only to be with Proud Eagle.

"I know a place where we can enjoy the tide and the moon without being disturbed," Proud Eagle said. "It is good that tonight is favorable, for so many recent nights have been so cold."

"I don't even have a wrap and I am comfortable," Billie said, then smiled seductively as she looked at

Proud Eagle. "But I believe it is you who have warmed me."

"I planned our evening together before the outdoor fire was built," he said, giving her a devilish grin.

Proud Eagle led her down to the beach, then took a sharp left and walked just past where the waning waterline left the rocks glistening in the moonlight.

When she saw a small makeshift rattan house, with a little fire burning before it, she gave Proud Eagle a look of wonder. "You built this for us?" she asked softly.

"Just for us," he said, whisking her up and into his arms. "Come. Warm blankets are spread on the sand inside the lodge. My woman, I thought of nothing else but this all day, these moments I will spend alone with you beneath the full moon and sparkling stars."

She clung to his neck as he lowered his lips to hers and gave her an all-consuming kiss.

He laid her gently on the pelts and blankets that he had placed there for her.

"When did you build this?" Billie asked as Proud Eagle knelt over her, slowly removing his clothes and tossing them aside.

"While you had the conference with Anna," he said, now nude.

He gently disrobed her and then knelt lower over her, their bodies touching.

"Do you approve?" he asked huskily.

"I could stay here forever if I could be with you," Billie murmured. She sucked in a breath when he swept his hand down and splayed his fingers across the center of her world at the juncture of her thighs, where she throbbed with need of him.

She closed her eyes and sighed as he began caressing her there, then tremored with passion when he sank a finger deep inside her and moved it within her in slow thrusts.

"Oh, what you do to me," she whispered against his cheek, a sudden curl of heat tightening her belly. "I am in heaven. Please, please kiss me."

His loins aflame, his manhood hard and ready as it lay against her thigh, his mouth seized hers with a passion that overwhelmed her, sending exquisite sensations spiraling through her body.

Shaken with desire, she clung to him, then made faint cries and drew him in as deeply as he wanted to go. He began his rhythmic strokes, each one taking her more deeply into the world that only he could create. He was the universe to her, the sun, the moon, the stars!

All distance that had ever been between them vanished.

"How I love you," she whispered against his lips. He ran a hand down her slim, sensuous body, then enfolded her with his solid strength as he moved with more speed within her.

In the fullness of his lust, he was aware of this

endlessly spiraling sweep of rapture that consumed him. Her mouth was so hot. Her lips tasted so sweet. Her shapely body was so pliant and willing in his arms.

He held her closely against him. Their bodies moved rhythmically together. His eyes were glazed with desire as he moved his lips away from hers so that he could look at her and see all the sweetness that was now his. He felt the curl of heat growing in his lower body.

His hand swept down her spine in a soft caress. Then he placed his hands beneath Billie's buttocks and tilted her body against his. Their heat mingled. Their moans filled the night air as once again they kissed, clung, and then went over the edge into a wonderful world.

When they came down from the clouds, Billie still held him. "I hate to let you go," she whispered against his lips. "Why can't we stay here forever? You are all I want in life. Only you."

"It is that way with me, as well, but I have duties that have been mine from the moment I took my first breath of life," Proud Eagle said. He leaned away from her, one hand on one of her breasts, gently kneading it. Her skin was so soft, it was as though it was dusted with pollen.

"When a son is born to a chief, his life's plan is already mapped out for him," he said. "For he, too, will one day be chief."

"And what a wonderful chief you are," Billie murmured. "One day we will also have a son, though Many Winds will be the next chief."

"And then his son will follow after him," Proud Eagle said, moving away from her.

He stared into the flames of the fire and thought he saw Many Winds' face. "I am proud to say that Many Winds is my son," he said. "When he becomes chief he will be bold and strong. He shall carry on my legacy and my father's, of long lasting peace for our people."

"Yes, there is the promise of a great leader in him," Billie said. "You have instilled so much in him already that speaks of the great chief he will be."

Proud Eagle took Billie's hands, urging her to sit beside him facing the small fire that burned just beyond the doorway of the tiny lodge. "It is good that you think so highly of my son. Soon he will be your son also," he said thickly.

He reached for a blanket and swept it around them both so that their naked shoulders touched beneath it.

"I will love being Many Winds' mother." Billie sighed. "It is so peaceful here. I hate having to return to my father's home and pack his things. It was so sad for me to have to do that with my mother's. It is just too final to discard one's clothes and other personal items."

"Life continues even when there is death," Proud Eagle said. "My woman, soon our lives will be combined as one, and all the darkness will be behind you."

He hung his head in silence.

She noticed and placed a finger beneath his chin, tilting his head so that their eyes could meet.

"For a moment you were gone from me," she said, searching his eyes in the firelight. "Were you thinking of another life? Another woman?"

"My wife was beautiful and sweet," he said thickly. "My world was torn apart when she was taken from me. I did not believe I could ever love again—not until you. Now the sadness that was in my heart has been replaced by your sunshine, but there are moments when I cannot help but to think of her."

"As it is only normal for you to do," Billie said softly. "I know that you must have loved her so. I would never be jealous of your memory."

"I do not think of her often anymore, but while planning our marriage, she has slipped into my mind more than once," Proud Eagle said. He put his arms around Billie and drew her close. They peered into the depths of each other's eyes. "You are all that I need in my heart now. You are everything to me. I cherish you, my woman. I will be everything for you."

Their lips met in a wondrous kiss.

Billie clung to him, feeling so fortunate to have met this man, even though their meeting had been under uncomfortable and strained circumstances.

She smiled as she recalled their heated exchange of words that day, while all along, they both had been suddenly attracted to one another.

"I will love you forever," she whispered against his lips. "I'll try not to disappoint you."

"You never could," he said, then swept the blanket from around them and spread her out beneath him again, to make slow, passionate love.

Chapter Thirty

As night fell outside, shrouding the mansion with a darkness that seemed all the more foreboding after what she had just read in her father's journals, Billie felt so disheartened that tears splashed from her eyes onto the desktop.

As she had read and reread the journals, she cringed as she discovered one discrepancy after another, proving that her father was a master at cheating not only the Makah but also those who worked for him.

She shoved the journals aside on his desk. She was bone-weary from it all.

Roy Clawson had not known that he had not lost as much at poker as he thought he had, for he had been cheated by her father.

"Father, I never knew you at all," Billie cried as she stared at a photo of him and her mother on his desk. "When did it start? How could Mother not have noticed?"

Suddenly a coldness seized her. Perhaps her mother had known the sort of man her father was.

Her mother must have been living in her own private, silent hell to know that she had married such a scoundrel.

Billie flinched when she thought of that first day when she had come to take over her father's duties. How cruel she had been to Proud Eagle! Was that inherited from her father?

But no! She had quickly regretted her behavior and had decided not to follow in her father's footsteps. She knew she had to make things up to Proud Eagle.

And she would, now that she had a chance. She would make up for all of the wrong her father had done to Proud Eagle and his people.

She shoved the chair back and rose quickly, determined to get past this fresh hurt.

She had come today to gather all of her father's belongings. Anna and Freda would arrive tomorrow to start preparing the huge house for the Makah children's school.

She had already packed her father's clothes in trunks, as well as anything else that was connected to him.

She had left the journals for last. They would be put in a separate trunk, ready to take to trial to prove Roy's guilt if it became necessary for her to testify.

She had left the one photo of her father and mother

on the desk, since she planned to take it with her into her marriage. But now after knowing the worst about her father, she would burn it. It stood for everything that was wrong.

She slid the photo free of the frame, walked to the fireplace, and fed it into the flames of the fire.

Needing a breath of air, she went to raise a window. She gasped when she saw a bright reflection of fire in the dark heavens.

And it came from the direction of Proud Eagle's village!

"Lord, no, no!" she screamed as she ran from the study.

She rushed out into the darkness and mounted her horse. Fear numbed her to the coldness surging against her face as she rode hard in the direction of the Makah village.

"How?" she whispered. "How could this happen?"

Her thoughts immediately went to Roy Clawson. No. He was behind bars.

It could be some of the lumberjacks that she had told that they no longer had a job. Could they have taken their anger out on the Makah, because they knew of her relationship with their chief?

She forced herself to stop the bombardment of thoughts and concentrate on getting to Proud Eagle's village so that she could help the people. She prayed no one had been harmed.

She pushed her strawberry roan into a harder gallop, until she was closer to the village, when she realized that the fire was not there. If it was, she would see it through the break in the trees.

She gazed up at the sky and saw that the reflection was brighter, which had to mean the fire, wherever it was, was at its peak.

She suddenly realized where the fire had to be. The trading post. It was in the same line of vision as the village.

She paled at the thought of something happening to Proud Eagle's cousin. It tore at her heart to think that Roy Clawson might have found a way to escape his cell and start the fire. He would surely make certain that Johnny Two Wings was left there to die in the flames.

Her heart pounding, Billie rode into the Makah village. Many warriors were mounting their steeds, with Proud Eagle in the lead.

"Proud Eagle!" Billie cried as she rode toward him.

He rode up and stopped beside her. "I fear it is the trading post," he said. "We are going to see if Johnny Two Wings is all right."

"I want to go with you," Billie said, determination in her voice. "If it is the trading post, I'm almost certain that Roy is involved. I have to know if he's escaped. If so . . ."

"If so, then he will pay," Proud Eagle said tightly. He looked over his shoulder at his warriors. "It is time to ride!"

The women and children of the village were huddled together in the moonlight as smoke drifted on the wind into the village.

Some men remained at the village, surely to protect them if by chance Roy had escaped the wrath of the flames and came to wreak more havoc on the Makah people.

She gave the women a lingering apologetic look. If her father hadn't brought his lumber company to Eagle Bay, none of these tragedies would have ever happened.

She hoped that they wouldn't hold her responsible for her father's crimes. In time, they would all know that she might be from her father's same blood, but she was nothing like him.

She stayed at Proud Eagle's side as they rode down to the beach and took the circuitous route to the trading post, instead of riding through the forest. There was nothing to hamper their speed as they rode beside the sea. And they could see just where the fire was burning. It definitely was the trading post.

The closer they came to it, the more smoke swirled toward them, choking Billie and stinging her eyes. As they approached, they could only hear the crackling of the flames, since the smoke made a screen they could no longer see through.

Billie said a little prayer for Johnny Two Wings. If he was trapped in that hellish fire, there would be no way that he would have survived.

Fighting their way through the smoke, they finally came to the smoldering remains of the trading post.

Cries of anguish came from those who knew Johnny Two Wings, for no one believed that he could have lived through this tragedy.

The trading post had been built of cedar—which had become aged and dry with time—and it would have gone quickly up in smoke once a fire got started.

Proud Eagle drew his horse to a halt, gave Billie a sorrowful glance, then dismounted.

She slid from her horse and ran with him up as close to the remains as possible.

Her heart stopped when she saw a man's body a few feet from the fire. The man was on his stomach, as though he had been crawling when he lost consciousness.

"Johnny Two Wings!" Proud Eagle cried as he ran toward him. He knelt down beside his cousin and slowly turned him over onto his back. Johnny Two Wings had no burns, though his face was blackened by the smoke. It was apparent that he had not been in the actual fire.

Johnny Two Wings began coughing and choking, grabbing at his chest. "My lungs . . . are . . . on fire," he gasped through his dried, black-encrusted lips. "It hurts!"

"You have inhaled too much smoke," Proud Eagle said. The relief he felt was evident in his eyes and voice. "You will be all right. I will take you home with me. Blue Cloud will care for you."

"Roy Clawson! He . . . did . . . this," Johnny Two

Wings said haltingly. He looked over at Billie. "He managed to get the keys and unlock the cell when I was outside getting firewood. When I came in, he was holding a broken lantern filled with kerosene and was tossing the liquid around onto everything. He did not even see me standing there because he was so intent on his mission. He tossed the lantern with its flame onto the kerosene-soaked desk. When he saw me, he stopped and started to give me a shove, but suddenly the flames set his clothes afire. The last thing I saw before the smoke engulfed me was Roy screaming and running from the building, his clothes aflame. A tongue of flame reached out and caught my pant legs on fire. I fell to the ground and rolled around until the flames were extinguished, then . . . then . . . began crawling. That's the last thing I can remember. The smoke was so thick in my lungs. I could no longer breathe."

"Lord!" Billie gasped, covering her mouth with a hand. "Thank goodness you are alive. But . . . surely Roy is dead."

"I will send warriors out in all directions to search for him," Proud Eagle said. "My first concern is you, Johnny Two Wings. I will get you home quickly."

He gazed closer into Johnny Two Wings' eyes. "Will it be too painful for you to ride?"

"My legs must have been burned for I feel pain there," Johnny Two Wings said. "But I can bear it enough to ride with you to the village."

"We can make a travois—" Proud Eagle said.

257

"I believe I can manage the pain enough without the aid of a travois, but thank you, cousin, for having such a big heart and for your care. I know I haven't had the chance to know you better," Johnny Two Wings said. "My mother never allowed me to know my father, but I have always been proud of the Makah in me. I never allowed her to take my heritage."

"You know that I have always seen you as family, no matter how much of your blood is white and no matter that you did not live among our Makah people," Proud Eagle said. "I knew your father. I never spoke of this before because you seemed happy with your life."

"You know my father?" Johnny Two Wings asked. "Who, Proud Eagle? Have I ever seen him? Has he ever been at my trading post?"

"Until a few years ago, yes, he was there often," Proud Eagle said, his voice grave. "A mud slide killed him."

"Yes, I remember the horrible mud slide that took so many people from your village," Johnny Two Wings said. "Then I shall never truly know him."

"You knew him very well," Proud Eagle said. He lowered his eyes momentarily, then looked at Johnny Two Wings again. "My father was your father."

"We are brothers?" Johnny Two Wings gasped, his eyes wide. "We have never been . . . cousins?"

"Our father confided in me a few short weeks before his death, but he asked me not to tell you, for he saw you as happy in the life that you had," Proud Eagle said. "I kept my promise to him—until now. It only seems right that you should know."

"We are brothers," Johnny Two Wings marveled, tears streaming from his eyes, making streaks through the black ash.

"Yes," Proud Eagle said.

"Your father—our father—was unfaithful to your mother?" Johnny Two Wings asked. "Your mother was so special. How could he . . . ?"

"Some men stray even if they have beautiful, sweet wives," Proud Eagle said. "It is not something that anyone can understand."

Billie was absorbing all that was being said. She was thinking about her own father's infidelity.

Was it possible that Proud Eagle could do the same to her? Did all men stray? Suddenly she did not feel all that confident about her forthcoming wedding.

As though Proud Eagle had read her thoughts, he looked over at her. "It shall never happen to you," he said sincerely. "My heart is yours forever. You believe that, do you not? You do not think that all men stray?"

"I hope not," Billie said, her voice catching.

"You must believe me," Proud Eagle said, searching her eyes. "We must enter into marriage with trust. Do you trust me?"

Tears splashed from Billie's eyes. "Yes, yes, I trust you. I shall never, ever doubt you."

Proud Eagle looked to his brother again. "Brother,

I will take you home now. My home is your home. My people are your people."

"Yes, take me home," Johnny Two Wings said, his eyes slowly closing. "I . . . am . . . so tired."

"Bring me a horse!" Proud Eagle called across his shoulder. His warriors were awaiting his instructions. "Then all but two of you search for the man who set this fire. Search for Roy Clawson!"

Everything happened fast then, and soon Billie was riding toward the village.

Johnny Two Wings was on a horse between her and Proud Eagle. She saw how Proud Eagle caught Johnny Two Wings more than once when he slumped over the saddle, for he would sometimes drift off to sleep, then awaken with a start.

Billie heard a noise to her left. Visions of Roy Clawson, burned and scarred, came to her mind as she looked toward the forest, where she had heard the sound. It was not far from where she was riding alongside the ocean.

She saw a deer, no doubt awakened by the commotion in the night, peering at her through the brush. In an instant it leaped away again into the dark shadows.

Billie knew that until Roy was found—dead or alive—she would not be able to feel certain that she was safe. She knew that if he was alive, he would be out for blood.

Hers!

Chapter Thirty-one

As Proud Eagle and his warriors scanned the forest for signs of Roy, Billie busied herself by helping to convert the mansion into a school.

The news about Johnny Two Wings was good. He had not been burned severely enough to leave any scars. He was at the village now, enjoying being with his clan for the first time in his life.

Proud Eagle was proud to share his life, his dreams, with the man he could now openly call his brother.

Anna was flitting around, rosy-cheeked and happy, as she instructed Billie as to what was necessary for teaching in each room. Freda and Sara were busy cleaning. The new school would open in two days.

First, though, something else very important was going to occur.

"I'm going to be married tomorrow, Anna," Billie said as she climbed the stairs with the headmistress. "My life has changed so quickly. Only a few months ago I was helping my mother in her millinery shop in Seattle. I didn't even have men on my mind, much less marriage."

"I knew that Proud Eagle was a strong, vital man when I first met him, on the day we gathered to make plans for the boarding school," Anna said. "It was easy to talk with him. I could tell that although he resented the interference of white people in his life, and his people's, he saw the importance of an education for the Makah children."

Billie paused on the second-floor landing. "He wants the next generation of Makah to be more knowledgeable than the last, so they will be able to fend off any attempts to cheat them. They will be able to go over new treaties and be able to stand up for their rights."

"Yes, I realize that," Anna said.

Sweat poured from her hair and across her brow, although outside it was a cool autumn day. The effort it was taking for her to help today was causing her obvious discomfort.

"And it will, in the end, benefit both the Makah and the United States government," she said breathlessly.

"Are you all right?" Billie asked, observing how hard Anna was breathing. She put a hand on Anna's arm gently and noted that the long sleeve was damp with perspiration.

"I guess I haven't done enough manual labor these past years," Anna said, laughing nervously. She brushed the sweat from her brow with her hand. "Sitting behind a desk is not the best way to get exercise."

Anna's condition took Billie back to the day when her mother had suffered a deadly heart attack. Right before Billie's eyes, her mother had dropped the hat she was decorating at the millinery shop and clutched her chest in desperation. Then, her eyes wild, her mother had fallen to the floor. With her last breaths, Billie's mother had told her that she loved her.

"Come with me," Billie said quickly, taking Anna's hand. "You need to rest. You've done all that you need to do today. Sara and Freda can do the rest. I need to go to my father's study and be certain I have removed everything so that it can now be yours."

"The oak desk is so grand," Anna said, walking stiffly down the long corridor toward the bedroom that had been assigned to her. "The books! Ah, the books in the library. I shall spend many hours reading. One never has enough knowledge, Billie. I guess you know that."

"Yes, that was what my mother always said," Billie murmured. "She saw to it that I got the best education, even though we both knew that I would be using my knowledge only to help her run a millinery shop."

"No education is ever wasted," Anna said as Billie stepped ahead of her and opened the door.

"As I said earlier, this bedroom was readied for

another woman, who never came to the mansion," Billie said, as she watched Anna go inside, her eyes wide.

"Your mother?" Anna asked, glancing at Billie. "You said that your father built the mansion and prepared this beautiful room in hopes that your mother would come from Seattle and live here."

"That's what he told me," Billie said, realizing as soon as the words slipped from her lips that she had spoken with the bitterness she felt in her heart.

"Oh?" Anna said.

Realizing that Billie seemed uncomfortable, Anna turned quickly away. She went over to the bed to run a hand over the spread. "This might be too beautiful for me," she said, her voice hushed. "It is so delicate. I have never been 'delicate.' "

"You are how you feel inside, not how you think others might perceive you," Billie said. She slid a comforting arm around Anna's waist. "Anna, this is yours. Please enjoy it. Mother would have adored it had she seen it. She loved lace and ruffles."

Billie gazed around the room herself. The sheer curtains at the two windows were lined with lace. The four-poster bed had a lovely canopy from which more lace dripped, trimmed with tiny pearls. The bedspread had beautiful white-embroidered flowers against a light pink background. It took one's breath away.

"Billie?" Sara's voice floated up the staircase from the downstairs.

"Excuse me, please," Billie said to Anna. She stood at the top of the stairs and called, "What is it, Sara?"

"We are almost finished down here. What else do you want me to do?" Sara asked.

"Please check the supplies in the kitchen and cellar so that we can be sure we have enough food to feed the children once school starts," Billie said. "We are planning to serve their morning and noon meals here."

"I don't have to do that, Billie," Sara replied. "It hasn't been too long since I traveled to Seattle and bought a good amount of supplies since I knew that winter was just around the corner. I have learned that the steamers stop coming this far until the next spring and one must prepare for the long siege."

"But is there enough for the children?" Billie questioned.

"What I had purchased would have been used for the lumberjacks. It will now be used for the children," Sara said. "There are adequate supplies."

"What do I smell coming from the kitchen?" Billie asked. "It smells delicious."

"Tomorrow is your wedding day," Sara said shyly. "It is traditional to have a lovely wedding cake, you know. So . . . I am preparing one especially for you."

"You are?" Billie said, then hurried down the stairs and hugged Sara. "Thank you, Sara. That is so sweet."

Sara returned the hug and smiled at Billie as she took her hands in hers. "Honey, I have waited for the day when I could make you a beautiful wedding cake," she said, tears shining in her eyes. "I have waited for the day I would see you walk down the aisle toward a handsome, wonderful man. Tomorrow is that day, Billie."

Billie's own eyes misted with tears. Then she laughed. "You have to know that my wedding won't be exactly as you envisioned it to be," she said. "I won't be walking down any aisle. There won't be any long candle tapers or huge bouquets of flowers in a church. The wedding ceremony will be simple, but one that I won't ever forget. I am getting the most wonderful man in the world. Isn't he the most handsome man you have ever seen?"

When Billie saw Sara's eyes waver, Billie knew that her thoughts had gone quickly to another man—the one she had loved.

Although Billie's father had lost his handsome face long ago from hard work and age, something about him had still made women almost swoon at first notice of him.

Billie had seen it from the time she was a child. Even when he was older, she had recognized it.

But Proud Eagle's handsomeness went much deeper than outward appearance. Not only was he handsome, he was a genuinely caring, loving, and giving person. He did not have a selfish bone in his body.

And this very morning, Billie had found one last

recent journal in her father's bedroom. The date of the last entry was the day before he had died.

She had almost cried with relief when she had read how her father had ordered Roy to cut the ropes that marked where he had planned to go farther into Makah territory. He had realized how wrong it was and he wanted Proud Eagle's respect.

Before he finished the entry, it looked as though someone interrupted him. Billie was certain that it had been Roy. She wondered if Roy had already set in motion his plan to kill her father.

All she knew was that for some reason her father had had a change of heart just before he had died.

Her memories of him would not be so sordid after all.

It made her head spin, though, that her father's journals showed such frequent changes of intent, like a chameleon changed colors. She would never know what had driven him to do any of the things he did.

It was good to know, though, that at the end he had tried to be someone she could love again.

"Billie?" Proud Eagle's voice called as he came into the foyer.

Billie smiled and her heart beat wildly as she ran to him and flung herself into his arms. "We were discussing our wedding," she said, gazing rapturously up at him, but Proud Eagle's body remained stiff. She grew somber and stepped away from him.

"Did you find him?" she asked, her voice drawn. "Did you find Roy?"

"There are no signs of him," Proud Eagle answered. "I know this land from end to end, and there are no signs of that man anywhere."

"He couldn't have just vanished," Billie said, disappointed and somewhat afraid. Roy was still out there, surely planning to kill her, and possibly Proud Eagle as well.

"Do you think he was burned so badly he might have rushed into the ocean to ease his pain, then never made it back to land?" Billie asked.

"It is something we might never know," Proud Eagle said.

Then he saw that the benches and desks from the boarding school had been placed in the parlor.

He smiled at Billie. "And so the school seems ready enough," he said. He gave Anna a wave as she came down the stairs.

"Yes, the exchange has been made, thanks to your warriors, who helped bring the desks and supplies in wagons to the new school," Anna said, sighing wearily. "It will be a wonderful place for the children to study and learn.

"And did you find that nasty man?" she asked.

"He seems to have escaped," Proud Eagle said tightly.

"Then let us all concentrate on something else," Anna said, smiling from Billie to Proud Eagle. "Let's just concentrate on that wedding tomorrow. It will be a grand day for us all."

"I'm so glad that you are coming," Billie said, hugging Anna.

"I'm not certain yet about Freda," Anna said. She gave Proud Eagle a look of apology. "That one is a marvelous teacher, but otherwise very shy. It's hard to get her out of her shell. But I shall try."

"It would be so nice to have everyone there," Billie said, then inhaled the wonderful fragrance of the cake that was baking in the kitchen.

She could tell that Sara had remembered her favorite. Chocolate!

She turned to Proud Eagle. "I'm finished here," she said. "I'm ready to go home, Proud Eagle."

They smiled over their shoulders at Anna and Sara, then went outside and mounted their horses.

"It's like a dream," Billie said, sidling her horse closer to Proud Eagle's. "Don't pinch me, darling. I'm afraid I would wake up and realize that none of this is real."

"I shall never, ever pinch you, then," Proud Eagle said, his eyes twinkling.

Chapter Thirty-two

The Makah men and women were in gala attire. Warriors had painted their bodies and now danced before a huge outdoor fire to the rhythmic throbbing of drums and rattles, leaping and bounding with feathered headgear waving.

Many women, with red-painted cheeks, and long, braided hair, sat in a semicircle away from everyone else, who sat back from them in a full circle.

These women joined the singing and rose to dance with the warriors as Billie sat beside Proud Eagle, both in their own special attire.

Billie wore a beautifully beaded doeskin dress that was heavily fringed at the skirt. She wore moccasins of the same doeskin and design, and her hair was adorned with a crown of tiny, colorful shells.

Proud Eagle wore the same sort of doeskin attire, as beaded and fringed as Billie's. His hair was loose and long down his back, a lone white eagle feather in a lock at the side.

Proud Eagle took one of Billie's hands and smiled

at her as she turned to him, the glow from the great fire leaping skyward reflecting in their eyes.

"You have made me very happy," Proud Eagle said quietly, so that only Billie could hear. "What you did for my son during the ceremony will never be forgotten. We both thank you."

Billie felt the heat of a blush and knew that her new husband spoke the compliment from his heart.

She brushed her fingers across his lips, her silent way of saying she loved and adored him.

Many Winds had gotten quite a surprise during the ceremony when Billie had turned to him and motioned for him to come to her.

She gently took him by the hand and led him to stand between herself and Proud Eagle.

She had then proceeded to include Many Winds in the ceremony, making promises to him, just as she had just done with his father.

Billie vowed to Many Winds that from this day forth she would be his mother and would care for him as though he had come from her own womb. She promised to be there for him on good and bad days.

As she vowed these things to Many Winds, she heard gasps of wonder from the Makah people. She gazed over at Proud Eagle and saw admiration reflected in his eyes. He was touched that his bride could be so thoughtful on what was seen as her special day.

Many Winds had burst into tears and flung himself

into Billie's arms. She had held him close, before he had turned to his father and clung to him for a moment. When he went back to sit with the other children, pride shone in his eyes.

Billie would never forget that sudden strengthening of the bond between herself and the child.

The ceremony was now behind them, and they were enjoying the celebration of love with the Makah community, and Sara, Anna, and Freda. Billie's cheeks ached from smiling so much as the dancing and singing continued.

She looked over at Johnny Two Wings, who sat with the other bachelors, his eyes filled with contentment and pride.

Once the dancers stopped, the games began. Filled with laughter and merriment, the people gathered on the beach, waiting for the warriors to line up on each side of a long rope. Billie ran beside Proud Eagle, who was expected to be a part of the tug-of-war game. This was one of the traditional Makah games.

Proud Eagle took his place in the sand, as others took theirs.

Shouts filled the air as the men grabbed the rope, with Proud Eagle leading one side and Johnny Two Wings leading the other. He smiled mischievously at Proud Eagle.

The tug-of-war began. There was much grunting and groaning and sweating, and feet slipping and sliding in the sand.

Billie clasped her hands excitedly as she watched

273

first her husband and then Johnny Two Wings struggle with the rope.

Proud Eagle looked as though he was about to lead his side to victory, then he slightly loosened his grip on his end of the rope—enough for Johnny Two Wings to suddenly take the victory away from him.

Proud Eagle recognized that his brother might need an extra boost of confidence. He wanted Johnny Two Wings to feel as if he belonged among the tribe.

Today was the beginning of Proud Eagle's attempt to make things up to his brother.

"Did you see that?" Many Winds said as he came to Billie's side.

Her eyes wavered and her heart skipped a beat, for she was afraid that Many Winds had seen the deception as well.

"See what?" she asked cautiously.

"My father! Johnny Two Wings' side beat my father's side," Many Winds said, his eyes wide. "My father rarely loses at anything."

"It is best to taste defeat sometimes in one's life to appreciate the winning better," Billie said, relieved to know that Many Winds hadn't seen exactly what had happened.

"One cannot count on winning every time," Proud Eagle said, coming to stand next to Many Winds. "You learn from losing."

"That is almost exactly what Billie told me," Many Winds said.

Proud Eagle drew Billie into his arms. "My woman can teach you a lot, my son," he said. "That is just one reason she will make you a good mother."

"The tide is now low, so we will have horse races," Proud Eagle said before leaving Billie to grab the reins as a young brave brought his horse to him.

He waited for his brother to be given a horse.

As the race began, Billie watched Proud Eagle and Johnny Two Wings, wondering how this challenge between brothers would end. Proud Eagle rode his steed valiantly and hard, and then Johnny Two Wings gained on him and passed him.

Then in one blink of an eye, Proud Eagle rode past his brother and won.

People cheered as he dismounted, but another race was already about to begin, drawing all attention there.

Proud Eagle and Johnny Two Wings gave their horses to a young brave, then stood with Billie, one on each side.

"My son looks so noble on his pony," Proud Eagle said, squaring his shoulders proudly as Many Winds prepared himself for his own race, while his opponent mounted another pony.

Their race began. Many Winds clung to his reins and stretched low over his pony's flying mane, his moccasined feet pounding the pony's sides. Only occasionally did he glance at his opponent, who was neck and neck with him.

And then one more sinking of his heels into the flanks of his mount and Many Winds passed the other young brave, laughing proudly when he realized that he had won.

All the children crowded around him as he dismounted, the young braves patting him on the shoulder admiringly, the young girls shyly watching.

And then Snow came bounding along the sand and leaped into Many Winds' arms, barking and licking his face.

"It is such a good day," one of the warriors said as he came and gave Proud Eagle a hug. "Congratulations, chief. I hope your days and nights will be filled with the same happiness I see in your eyes at this moment."

Others came along with the same sort of congratulations, as the women hugged and made comments to Billie that let her know she had been accepted into their clan of Makah.

She was bursting with happiness and pride. It was a day she would cherish into old age, when she could look back and relive these moments with a smile on her face and a song in her heart.

"There is one other thing!" Proud Eagle said, as he gazed around at his people who were crowded around him on the beach.

He took Billie by a hand and pulled her around in front of him.

"My woman, my wife, you have said that you feel that your name is not feminine enough," he said. "I have brought you a new name today into our marriage, if you would want it."

"You have?" Billie asked, pleasantly surprised. "What is it?"

"Pretty Rain," Proud Eagle said, holding both of her hands. "We came together finally as friends, as allies, in the rain on the day of the mud slide. I saw you that day as pretty in the rain. My wife, do you accept the name?"

She flung herself into his arms, tears shining in her eyes. "Yes! I adore my new name. I adore you."

Thunderous applause broke out and shouts of approval. "This is a good time for our feast!" one of the women in the crowd cried. "Come, let us eat before our chief and his wife depart from us for the rest of the night!"

Everyone eagerly made their way over to where wooden platters were stacked and where large pots of food sat around the edges of the fire, ready for eating.

But the thing that stood out and made Billie stop and gasp was the three-tiered wedding cake that Sara had made for her.

The chocolate cake was covered with rich, wonderful chocolate icing, with tiny, beautifully shaped flower rosettes in pinks and greens covering the top.

"I have never seen anything as beautiful!" Billie exclaimed, clasping her hands in delight as she stared in amazement at the cake.

"I promised you a wedding cake," Sara said, moving to Billie's side, "and I made one that I knew you would love. Chocolate was always your favorite when you were a child."

"And look how you have decorated it," Billie marveled. "I remember other cakes that you made when I was small, but I cannot recall any as lovely as this."

She gave her a warm hug. "Thank you, Sara," she said, her voice breaking. "And—and—, Sara, I love you. Truly I do."

"I hoped that you could get past . . ." Sara was unable to finish her statement. "I love you dearly, Billie. Congratulations. You have married a special man."

"Yes, I know," Billie said, smiling contentedly as she drew away from Sara and gazed at Proud Eagle. "How did I get so lucky?"

"I love your new name," Sara said, giving Proud Eagle a smile. "He adores you, Billie."

"I love my new name, too, and I am so in love with my husband," Billie said.

"And that you included Many Winds in the ceremony let everyone know the sort of woman their chief has married," Sara said, then stepped aside when Proud Eagle came to admire the cake.

"My people are not familiar with cake," he said, his eyes taking in the confection. "It seems magical to their eyes."

"Wait until they taste it," Billie said, giggling.

Sara handed Billie a knife. "It's time for the bride and groom to cut the first piece, don't you think?" her eyes glowing with happiness.

"Yes, I do believe so," Billie said, giving her husband a sort of sly smile. "Are you ready to help me?"

Proud Eagle nodded and gripped the handle of the knife as Billie showed him how it should be done.

After the cake was sliced, Billie plucked a piece out from the rest.

"We are to feed each other a piece of the cake before anyone else gets any," she whispered, noticing how his eyes were dancing at this unusual custom.

They fed each other bits of the cake, smearing their faces with icing, and then everyone came for a piece of the delicious treat.

After the cake was eaten and appreciated, everyone piled the "real" food onto the wooden plates.

There was a vast abundance of foods, including all sorts of fish and shellfish, oil, starchy roots, berries, and a multitude of relishes and side dishes.

This time Billie didn't hesitate to eat the dogfish shark livers or toasted fish fins and gills. She knew that in time she would learn to enjoy all of the other varieties of food that the Makah brought in from the sea and harvested from the forest.

Anna had asked several of the children if they would like to see the school and have what she called a "sleepover." She promised it would be much different from the times when they were forced to sleep at the boarding school. She had games planned and treats for them to eat.

She had made up cots in the study, where a great fire would be burning in the fireplace. She had promised them stories and big bowls of popped corn before they went to their cots for the night.

Tomorrow true school would begin again, and the children would be returning home after their studies.

And just as most people had gotten their fill of the special foods of this celebration, Billie noticed that several warriors had hurried away and had gathered in a circle close to the beach.

"What are they doing?" Billie asked, watching their game, which she did not recognize. She was glad that her husband wasn't lured to join them, for she expected that soon the two of them would escape the celebration and retreat to their longhouse for a full night of lovemaking.

"They are playing a favorite game of our people," Proud Eagle told Billie in explanation. "It is called siahal. A member of one team conceals two bones, one marked and one unmarked, and the opposing team guesses which hand holds the unmarked one. There will be much excitement as the teams vie for high stakes and try to outwit each other. Soon you will hear drums and singing. While a man has the bone, his team members sing and beat drums to increase his powers of deception. The sticks you see in the sand are counters for keeping score."

"Do you want to join them?" Billie asked, after hearing the excitement in her husband's voice as he explained the game to her.

Proud Eagle turned to her with an all-knowing smile, making her shiver with anticipation.

"You don't need to answer," she said, giggling.

With that, they saw that everyone was involved in playing or watching the game. They realized that this was the moment to slip away.

Smiling and holding hands, they ran to the long-house, then locked the door behind them.

They undressed each other quickly, then moved to the thick pallet of furs that Proud Eagle had placed in front of the fireplace before they had joined each other outside for the ceremony and celebration.

The fire had burned to low embers, casting a soft glow around the room as Billie and Proud Eagle re-discovered the wonders of lovemaking.

He bent over her and pressed his lips softly against hers, their bodies touching, their hands clasped above her head as Billie lay on her back beneath him.

Proud Eagle kissed her with an easy sureness, then leaned away from her and ran his hands down her body, taking in the roundness and stroking her curves.

Then he bent low over her again, his tongue brushing her lips lightly. Moving slowly, with deliberation, he allowed his manhood to touch her hot, moist center. Then he sank his heat deeply inside her.

Erotic warmth knifed through Billie's body, stabbing deeply within her, the hot, demanding pleasure gripping her.

Proud Eagle brushed each of her breasts with kisses and flicks of his tongue, then caressed and cupped them in his hands.

She twined her arms around his neck, and then her legs around his waist, bringing him even more deeply inside her.

As before, she found herself lost to him as waves of ecstasy washed through her body.

Proud Eagle cradled her close, their bodies rocking together, swaying, plunging, singing!

"My Pretty Rain," Proud Eagle whispered huskily against Billie's lips.

Again he kissed her, and she felt his hunger in the hard, seeking pressure of his lips. She felt her own as she cried out to reach the pinnacle of passion with him.

The pressure was building somewhere deep inside her. It grew hotter and hotter, like fire was consuming her.

Billie's body stiffened. She arched her back as she gazed up at Proud Eagle with passion-clouded eyes.

"I want you, oh, how I need you," she whispered, her cheeks hot.

"As I want you," Proud Eagle said. "You are mine, for always."

"For always," Billie whispered against his lips. "For . . . always . . ."

They clung.

They kissed.

They came to that place that they discovered only in one another's arms. It was a fulfillment so complete, they could only sigh in utter pleasure against each other's lips . . .

Chapter Thirty-three

"This night is what dreams are made of," Billie murmured as she lay beside Proud Eagle, content, fulfilled, and marvelously in love. "And thank you for my beautiful new name. I love it. Pretty Rain. It is perfect. But it will take time for me to get used to it. I have been known as Billie for too long to suddenly be someone else."

"You do not have to worry about it until you yourself feel ready to use the new name," Proud Eagle said. He sat up beside her as she lay on the thick pelts beside the fire.

"I think I would rather wait until your people know me better, and then I will feel comfortable to be called by my new name," Billie said, leaning up on an elbow to smile up at him.

"You are so pretty, my wife," Proud Eagle said, running his fingers through her hair. "My woman with sunshine hair. My beautiful Billie Pretty Rain."

Billie laughed softly at the name, but she was glad that he understood why she needed to be known by the name her parents had given her for just a little while longer.

"Finally I have new growth at the roots," Billie said, sighing. "I regret so much having cut my hair, but at the time I felt compelled to follow in my father's footsteps. To do so, I felt, I had to do what I could to fit in with the men."

"But you are not a man," Proud Eagle said, leaning down and brushing his lips across her brow.

He then ran a hand across her stomach, causing something inside her to flutter sensually.

"You are all woman," he said huskily, then kissed his way down from her breasts to where she was alive again with want of him.

Then he gave her a smile as he sat up and took her hands. "I would like to take you someplace and show you something," he said. "Then we can return and make love again and again."

Billie sat up, her eyes wide with a question.

"Trust me," he said. "Come, then you will see."

"You know that I trust you in everything," Billie said.

As she slid into her clothes she watched him dress in full buckskin.

When she was fully clothed, he handed her the same warm sealskin cloak that she had worn that day after they had swum to and from the cave.

"It is cold outside now," Proud Eagle said, putting on a cloak himself. "It will be especially cold on horses, and we must travel a ways to get to where I want to take you."

"Aren't you going to tell . . ." Billie asked as he took her hands and urged her to her feet.

"I would rather wait and let you see for yourself," Proud Eagle said.

He drew her into his arms and nuzzled her neck, then kissed her lips, hers hungry with passion beneath his, but then he stepped away from her.

"The moon is bright tonight," he said, opening the door. "It will lead us safely to where I am taking you."

Proud Eagle took her by the hand and walked with her to his corral. Soon their horses were saddled and ready for riding. Billie felt the chill of the night on her face as she rode away from the village with Proud Eagle close enough beside her that she felt safe. There was just something about him that made her always feel comforted and loved.

She realized right away that he was taking her in the direction of the mansion, which was now called White Owl School, in honor of the White Owl Clan of Makah.

It made her heart swell with pride to know that she had given something special to the Makah children.

"We are almost there," Proud Eagle said, giving Billie a smiling glance. "You do know where we are going?"

"Yes, but I just don't know why," Billie said, already seeing the shine of lamplight in the windows up ahead and smelling the smoke from the fireplaces.

"After I tell you, I do not think you will mind leaving our bed on our wedding night," Proud Eagle said.

"And so you are now going to tell me?" Billie asked.

The moon was shining down onto Proud Eagle's copper face as they rode beside the calm ocean. Billie saw again his sculpted features and his absolute handsomeness. It was a face of love and compassion, a face she loved to touch and kiss.

Billie drew a tight rein beside Proud Eagle in front of the White Owl School. Warmth seemed to radiate from the windows, especially from what had only recently been the large parlor, as not only lamplight shone through them, but also the glow of the fire in the huge fireplace.

"I wanted to show you something special that is happening even now for my people's children. The smaller ones that will not attend the school for a few more winters were given permission to come and spend the night with their older brothers and sisters and cousins," Proud Eagle said, not yet dismounting, but instead looking at Billie from his saddle.

"You wanted to show me something that has to do with the children," Billie said. "You know how I adore them. You were right to think that I would be curious about what is happening tonight."

"Come into the house, then," Proud Eagle said, and they dismounted.

They then walked hand in hand, up the steps and into the foyer.

Candles in wall sconces lit the entryway, and the huge staircase. She caught the smell of the popped corn that Sara and Anna had served the children.

Children's laughter rang down the long corridor from the parlor, making Billie wonder what was happening that Proud Eagle felt was so special that he brought her there at this time of night.

As Proud Eagle and Billie walked toward the parlor, she heard a deep, gruff voice. It was old.

The closer she came to the parlor and listened, the more she realized she recognized the voice. It was the shaman!

She looked quickly over at Proud Eagle. "Blue Cloud is here? Is someone ill? Oh, surely not Many Winds!"

"No, no one is ill, my wife. Blue Cloud is not only our people's shaman. He is also our clan's storyteller," Proud Eagle said, his eyes dancing in the candles' glow.

"Storyteller?" Billie said, her eyes widening. "He's here telling stories to the children?"

"Yes," Proud Eagle said, stopping just outside the parlor door.

"Children love to hear stories," Billie said, lowering her voice so that their presence would not be known just yet.

"Yes, they love to hear stories, but my choice of where they would hear these stories tonight, and by whom, is what makes the difference," Proud Eagle said, pride in his voice. "Schooling in the white man's way is required of our children, is it not?"

"Yes . . ."

"No one said that they cannot also be taught things by a Makah teacher, did they?" Proud Eagle said.

"No, but I thought that the government purposely kept your people's heritage out of the school," Billie replied.

"Anna spoke on the children's behalf. She saw that this is the right thing for the children," Proud Eagle said. "Storytelling has always been revered by Makah children. Storytellers not only fascinate, but they educate. Our storyteller will come once a week and sit with the children to teach the stories and myths of our people."

"What a wonderful thing for the children," Billie said, truly awed by the plan.

He took Billie's hand. "Come inside," he said. "I believe Blue Cloud is just ending one story and will soon begin another, perhaps his last for the night. The children's beds await them. They will go to bed tonight with not only thoughts of today's fun but also stories of their people on their minds."

The door was at the back of the room where the children were sitting on the floor, caught up in listening to Blue Cloud, who sat on a blanket facing them. Billie crept into the room alongside Proud Eagle.

Huge bowls sat among the children, the popped corn almost emptied from each now. Some children reached in and took a handful, but their eyes never left Blue Cloud. Billie's own eyes searched for her new son. She found Many Winds sitting with some of his special friends.

"Let us sit," Proud Eagle whispered to Billie. "Let us enjoy the tales as well."

Billie nodded, then sat down in a chair at the back.

She saw Anna and Freda sitting in the darker shadows of the room. Their eyes were on Blue Cloud, and the two women were seemingly as taken by his tales as the children were.

"Children, you have heard the dogs howl at night. You have wondered why they do that, have you not?" Blue Cloud asked, his old eyes moving from child to child, smiling as they all eagerly answered "yes" together.

"Children, the dogs are howling at the Dog Star. The dogs believe they have relatives living on the Dog Star, and they speak to them with loud voices. Sometimes the Dog Star comes close to the earth, and then the dogs and wolves howl into the night, for they believe they should speak to their people on the star whenever they are near enough to hear their voices."

He paused and smiled. "And so, children, we

should not complain. You should never object when your dogs howl at night, for you know now why they do it, and you know that they were told to do it by a voice greater than man's, do you not?"

"Yes!" the children responded loudly.

"I have one more tale, and then it will be time for me to go. But before I leave, listen. Hear about one night when I was a child your age, when I had a dream," Blue Cloud said.

His old eyes mesmerized his young audience as his gaze moved from child to child. He wore a long robe, and his long gray hair hung in two braids across his shoulders.

"In this dream an otter came to me and told me that I had an owl on the roof of my longhouse, but when I went there I did not see it," Blue Cloud said. "The otter left me, and I saw him dig a hole in the ground near the roots of a pine tree. While digging, he found a feather. He brought the feather to me. He again told me that there was an owl on my roof. Again I looked and did not see. The otter went away and left me alone. In my dream, I went back to my bed. But I was disturbed by this cry—*Whoooo-whooooo-who-who*. I looked up and saw an owl in my longhouse. It was above me, sitting on a rafter. I quickly discovered that the feather the otter had dug up was lying on my breast. The owl spoke to me. It said the feather was from the wing of the powerful, mystical Thunder Bird. As soon as I sat up, both the owl and the feather flew from my longhouse and up

290

into the sky. I was afraid, but again I slept. When I finally awakened from the dream, the sun was in the sky, warming the world. A butterfly flew into my longhouse and settled upon my hand. The butterfly fanned me for a moment with its lovely yellow wings, then took flight and I never saw it again. The owl and the otter never returned in my dreams. I wondered what it all meant?"

"What did it mean?" the children asked almost in unison when Blue Cloud paused in his tale, as though he awaited the children's question.

He looked around the room. "What did it mean?" he said, his voice filled with humor. "Nothing special. But know that what is to be, will be."

A silence ensued as the children gazed captivated at the old shaman storyteller, who had skillfully told them several tales tonight, most of which left them in deep thought.

Proud Eagle urged Billie to follow him from the room.

"The children were so absorbed in Blue Cloud's tales," Billie murmured as she and Proud Eagle hurried from the mansion, without anyone realizing they had come and gone.

Her eyebrows arched as she took her reins and mounted her strawberry roan. "Did you understand what the story was about? What was the reason for it? Was there something in it that I did not understand?"

"Often the stories confuse, but in time they are

logical," Proud Eagle said. "That is why the storytellers are clever and good. They make one think. And
thinking is what makes one learn."

"I watched Many Winds while Blue Cloud was
telling the story," Billie said. "He was totally involved. I watched his eyes. He was taking it all in."

"He will go to bed tonight with the stories on his
mind and perhaps he will dream of owls, otters, and
butterflies," Proud Eagle said, chuckling.

The mansion far behind them now, they rode along
the ocean again in the bright moonlight. "I feel so
content tonight," Billie said, sighing with pleasure.

Just as she said it, she heard a sound on her left
side, in the darker shadows of the forest.

"Proud Eagle, did you hear that?" Billie said
tensely, sidling her horse closer to his. "Did you hear
something like . . . a groan?"

He started to tell her that he hadn't, then he, too,
heard it. His eyes narrowed as he gazed in the direction from which it came.

"We should stop and search for what is making
the sound," Proud Eagle said, drawing a tight rein.
Billie followed his lead.

Proud Eagle took a knife from his saddlebag and
crept toward the shadows. As he approached, it
sounded more like a baby crying than moaning.

Billie heard it too.

"Someone is hurt," she said. She stepped closer to
Proud Eagle. "It . . . might . . . be Roy. If it is, he is
in terrible pain."

"Or he might not be. He might be pretending," Proud Eagle said thoughtfully. "But, no. I do not really expect to find Roy alive. Let us find who needs our assistance."

They hurried into the outer fringes of the forest, then stopped in their tracks when they saw what awaited them there . . .

Chapter Thirty-four

"It's only a bear cub," Billie gasped in relief as she gazed down at the little animal tangled up in bushes by its hind leg. "I had feared . . ."

"Do not feel all that relieved," Proud Eagle said, looking cautiously around him. "Where there is a cub, there is also a mother. We must untangle the cub quickly and send it on its way. If we do not put distance between us and the cub, we might wrongly become the target of the mother's rage."

Billie paled. With a pounding heart, she watched Proud Eagle fall to his knees and begin cutting through the tangled brush in an effort to free the cub, whose dark eyes watched him. "I almost have it," he said, occasionally scanning in the denser shadows for the mother.

He continued cutting, then flinched when he heard a loud growl that sounded like thunder coming from the darkness toward them.

"Lord, no," Billie whispered. "Proud Eagle, how close do you think she is?"

"Too close," Proud Eagle said, rising quickly as the last of the limbs fell away from the cub.

He took Billie's arm. "Walk slowly, yet deliberately," he urged her. "We do not want to draw undue attention by running. A bear senses fear. She might chase us for that reason alone."

"But . . . we were helping the cub, not harming it," Billie said, every step a shaky one.

"The bear does not have the same sense of logic as humans," Proud Eagle said, not taking the time to look over his shoulder to see where the bear might or might not be. "It has no idea whether or not we caused its cub distress. We must get on our horses and get as far away as possible as quickly as we can."

A loud roar came to them, and then a soft sort of snuffling sound that might mean that the mother had found her cub.

"Mount your horse without a sound," Proud Eagle urged Billie as he mounted his own. "Ride away at a slow lope unless you hear the bear approaching. If you do, then ride hard, Billie. I will be close. I will not let her attack you."

Billie said nothing. She was concentrating only on escaping. When both she and Proud Eagle were far away from the danger, they laughed with relief.

Billie was glad when they reached the safety of the longhouse and the door was locked behind her and her husband.

Snow came bounding from the back rooms, where he had been sleeping on Many Winds' bed.

"And so now you are awake, are you?" Proud Eagle said, stooping and catching Snow as he leaped into his arms.

Proud Eagle snuggled him close. "You miss Many Winds, don't you, Snow? I wish I could make you understand that there will be no more nights without him. Tonight is the last. Then he will be home to snuggle in his bed with you."

Snow barked as though he knew what Proud Eagle had said, then jumped down and retreated once again to Many Winds' room.

"His white fur is so thick and beautiful," Billie murmured as she slid the cloak from around her shoulders and Proud Eagle removed his own.

"In the spring you will see how his fur is used to benefit our people," Proud Eagle said. He slid his arms around Billie's waist and drew her close to him.

He kissed her passionately, then swept her up and carried her to their pallet and laid her down on the plush furs and blankets there.

"Wife, the night is young," he said huskily. "Shall we resume what we did not finish earlier? Or are you too tired?"

"I will never be too tired to make love with you," Billie murmured as he was already lifting the dress over her head. "I have heard that sometimes women make excuses of having a headache or other ailments.

Some see lovemaking as a chore. I see it as something wonderful."

"That is because you have sensual feelings that many women do not have," Proud Eagle said.

Soon she lay naked before his feasting eyes. He slowly ran his hands down her body, until he came to the soft patch of hair between her thighs.

When he gently stroked her womanhood with his fingers, he saw fire leap into her eyes. It set his loins aflame with need.

"I do . . . feel . . . sensual," Billie said.

She moaned and closed her eyes when Proud Eagle leaned low over her and replaced his fingers with his tongue. She felt herself melting as he pressed a warm kiss.

Billie was shocked at the intensity of the feelings that were overwhelming her. A sudden curl of heat tightened her belly when his tongue caressed her again. Her eyes filled with the awareness of his body as he stood over her and disrobed.

He stretched out over her. She wrapped her arms around his neck and clung to him as their bodies joined hungrily.

He gave her a fierce, fevered kiss, and her thoughts grew hazy with pleasure.

As his kiss deepened, her blood surged in a wild thrill as never before. Her head began to reel with the intensity of her feelings. She trembled as her body yearned for the fulfillment she knew was near. She could feel the urgency building.

"My woman, my wife," Proud Eagle whispered against her lips, himself filled with an almost unbearable passion. He kissed the soft hollow of her throat, then flicked his tongue across the nipple of one breast, and the other.

He leaned away from her and paused for a moment just to gaze down at her with burning eyes. Then his mouth covered hers again with a fiery kiss, just as he felt the wondrous release that overwhelmed him.

When she moaned with ecstasy and pressed even closer to his hard, muscled body, he knew that she, too, had found the ultimate pleasure once again within his arms.

Breathing hard, they clung together for a moment longer, then Proud Eagle rolled away from her and stretched out on his back, his eyes never leaving her.

"You are even more beautiful after making love," he said, one of his hands playing with her ringlets of hair. "I can see in your eyes that you take much pleasure from our lovemaking."

"As I see it in yours," Billie murmured. She touched his face and ran her fingers across his sculpted lips. "You have given me so much. Had I never met you . . ."

She shook her head. "No, I won't even think about that," she said. "We did meet. We fell in love. And now we are man and wife with a wonderful future ahead of us."

She sat up and gazed into the fire. "I wonder how

long it will take me to get pregnant," she said, then smiled as he sat next to her, their bare hips touching. "I want more than one child. I want many! I was an only child, and I would never wish that on anyone. I was so lonely at times. I found myself pretending that I had a sister."

"And what did you name your pretend sister?" Proud Eagle asked enjoying this new side of his woman.

"Baby Cinnamon," Billie said, giggling. "She and I went on many adventures together. When I rode my horse, she was on one of her own, riding alongside me. When I played with my dolls, I made certain she had one of her own to play with. Even our dolls talked to each other. We made mud pies together . . ."

"You are indeed a woman of much imagination," Proud Eagle said. "I like that."

"I loved the cinnamon that Sara put in the cookies she made for me," Billie said. "That is how I chose the name."

She moved to her knees before him. "Then can we have several children?"

He took her hands in his. "Many Winds has felt the same feelings as you and has asked over and over again when I would marry so that he could have a brother or sister, so, yes, my wife, we shall have as many children as you wish."

She flung herself into his arms. "Thank you," she said, joyful tears springing to her eyes. "You have already given me so much, and now you are giving me more."

"You have given twofold to me what I have given you," he said. He laid her on her back, then moved atop her again. "I want to give more to you this night. I want to give you all the love that I can bring from my heart. I want to give you my seed so that it can start growing into a child in your womb."

Again they made love, but this time it was slow and easy so that every moment was savored.

"Oh, what you are doing to me," Billie whispered against his lips. "Please, oh, please . . . never . . . stop . . ."

Chapter Thirty-five

Happy and content, Billie had found the last five months rewarding as she blended in quickly with the Makah women, learning their ways. Even now, a cradle made from cedar bark was suspended from the rafter of her home, awaiting the arrival of her and Proud Eagle's baby.

She was in her first four months of pregnancy. After the birth, on days when she would be sitting before the fire, sewing or reading, she would be able to rock the babe by a cord that would run from the cradle to one of her feet. She had been shown how to make a cedar bark hood for her child that would protect its face from insects and light.

Pounded cedar bark also served as diapers!

Cedar bark was the mainstay of basketry as well. She had been taught that it would be stripped from the young trees when the sap rose in spring, allowing it to be easily pulled free. Only the smooth inner bark would be taken home. It was dried, then folded and stored. In weaving, a woman could split strips of whatever thickness and width she needed.

Today she sat alone in her longhouse, in a rocking chair that she had brought from the mansion, embroidering a design on a small woven basket that she was proud to say she had made.

She paused long enough to reach up and run her fingers through her hair, thankful that it had finally grown long enough for her to look more like herself. She could hardly wait for it to be long enough to braid.

She looked toward the window, where sun poured through the glass. Proud Eagle and his men were felling trees early in the cutting season, since the snows had not been harsh enough this winter to keep them totally away from the forest.

The women would meet occasionally in groups in one another's longhouses to work on their basketry, but usually they met at the council house so the children could join them and play.

Billie sat among them, knowledgeable enough of basket weaving to sell her work at the trading post. The basket she was presently making could be sold for twenty-five or fifty cents worth of goods, such as rolled oats.

She enjoyed going to the trading post, for it was always good to see Johnny Two Wings. Although he came to the village often to be among his people, it was never enough for Proud Eagle, now that he openly accepted Johnny Two Wings as his brother.

Proud Eagle enjoyed the moments they shared when they could talk of family.

Johnny Two Wings' mother lived in Seattle and never stepped on Makah soil. She was married now to a rich trapper and had two small children. Johnny Two Wings never visited them. He was content to be who he was, without her interference.

He was rebuilding his trading post and filling it once again with things that would benefit the Makah as trading goods. He had just begun to court a woman from another Makah clan, so Proud Eagle looked forward to being a proud uncle someday.

Billie felt a moment of dizziness, which had only recently begun to plague her. Earlier in her pregnancy, she had suffered terribly with morning sickness.

She set her embroidery work aside on a table, closed her eyes, and ceased rocking until the dizziness passed. She had questioned the other women about such a feeling, and they had reassured her that when one was with child many things could trouble her.

She wanted to do nothing that might cause her to lose this child. She hoped that these problems were not a warning that she might not be able to have any more children.

She would always think back to her mother and how she had been advised not to have more than one child. It would devastate Billie if she was told the same thing!

She would feel that she had let her husband down, for she knew that he also was eager to have more children. And she knew that Many Winds wished to have many brothers and sisters.

"I won't let either of you down," she whispered to herself.

The dizziness passed, and Billie picked up her basket to resume embroidering a design of spring flowers on its side. The Makah basket makers had developed the art of fine-wrapped twining to produce round or oval baskets with designs made from brightly colored grasses set against a background of creamy white bear grass.

She knew that these particular baskets were extremely popular among white people and neighboring Indian groups and were produced in astonishing numbers at Proud Eagle's Makah village. Half of the baskets made there were sold through Johnny Two Wings' trading post, and the rest were taken to Seattle.

She planned to sew many cattail seed beads, as well as gull bones and feathers, on her basket once the embroidery work was finished, to complete its special look.

She missed working with the other women, who were in the large council house today, but since she felt so strange, she wanted to stay near her bed. There would always be another day to join them.

Dizzy again, Billie heaved a sigh and set her work

aside, then rose slowly from the chair and went to her bedroom.

The warmth from the fireplace in the large room wafted into the bedroom, as Billie lay down on the bed.

She rested her head on a pillow and drew a blanket up over her just above her belly, which was only now beginning to show her pregnancy. Just as she got comfortable, warm, and ready to take a nap, she heard a sound in the outer room.

"Proud Eagle, is that you?" she called, surprised that he could have finished his work this early. Usually the men stayed in the forest until late afternoon.

When there was no response, Billie settled down again on the bed thinking that perhaps along with everything else that had plagued her in her early pregnancy were sounds that were not truly there.

She again closed her eyes and felt herself drifting off to sleep.

She awakened with a start when she heard a sound again. This time she knew that it was not her imagination. Someone had knocked something over in the outer room.

Her heart began pounding with a sudden fear as she heard footsteps.

"Proud Eagle, please tell me if it's you," she said, sliding off the bed.

She hung her head when another dizzy spell seized her.

When she opened her eyes, she saw leather boots. Whoever was standing there was close to her, and her heart skipped a beat. Proud Eagle never wore boots.

She looked up into a face that she hardly recognized, yet she could identify it from the lifeless gray eyes and bald head.

"You!" she gasped as she stared up at the grotesque face, terribly scarred from the fire at the trading post.

"Roy Clawson," she said, petrified that he was there and Proud Eagle wasn't.

And in her delicate condition she knew that she could not fight the man. She was at his mercy.

"You thought I'd died as a result of my burns, didn't'cha?" Roy said, holding a rifle steady on her.

"When no one could find you, yes, we thought you had died," Billie said tightly. "How did you survive? Your face . . ."

"Ain't a pretty sight, is it?" Roy said, frowning as he ran his free hand over the reddish-purple scars. "If it hadn't been for my aunt, I'd not have made it. But after I managed to get to Seattle as a stowaway on a steamer, she cared for me. Except for my scars, I'm as good as new . . . and ready to take back what's mine."

"And that is?" Billie asked. She knew that he could end her life, and her baby's, at any moment, so she stalled for time.

Proud Eagle was her only chance for survival, yet

he was in the forest and couldn't save her from a horrible fate at the hands of this crazed man.

"I've come for a purpose, so don't fret so much over my being here," Roy said, slightly lowering his rifle.

"And that is?" Billie asked, her eyes never leaving his.

"I heard that you married Proud Eagle and were living with him here," Roy said. "So that leaves the mansion empty, doesn't it?"

"I wasn't about to sell it to more white people so that they could interfere in the lives of the Makah," Billie said, slowly seeing a way to possibly trick Roy so that she might be saved from his wrath after all.

It was obvious that he didn't know about the change at the house.

Although he had heard about her marriage to Proud Eagle, it seemed that no one saw any importance in the mansion being used as a school for the Makah children. As far as Roy was concerned, the house still stood empty, the ghosts of the past its only occupants.

"I knew you wouldn't," Roy said. "You're coming with me to the house, and you'll sign the lumber business over to me. If you refuse to do this, I'll not only kill you, I'll ambush Proud Eagle and kill him."

"Why didn't you just go to the mansion and get the papers yourself?" Billie asked, raising her eyebrows.

"Only you know where they are," Roy said, his

eyes narrowing angrily. "They might even be here."
He leaned closer to her. "Are they? Are they here?"

"No, I didn't bring anything from the lumber business into my marriage," Billie said, her pulse racing
at the opportunity of getting Roy out to exactly
where she knew Proud Eagle was.

"I knew you wouldn't," Roy repeated.

"But you could have gone and looked through
things and found them without my help," Billie said,
playing into his hands by letting him think that there
could be such papers to turn over to him, when, in
truth, there were not. She had sent all of her father's
journals and papers of ownership to Seattle, where
they now lay safely in a bank vault.

"Do you think I'd ever dare try and claim that
business as mine without your signature?" Roy said.
"Come on, Billie Boy. Let's get outta here before your
husband comes home and finds me here."

"When he finds me gone, he'll be out for your
blood, Roy," Billie said. "And, Roy, how on earth do
you think signing a few papers can get you
anything?"

"Because once I have them papers in my hands, I
can go to Seattle and register the ownership. Then
just let anyone try and stop me from cutting those
trees." Roy motioned with his rifle toward the door.
"Come on. Grab a wrap. We're going for a ride."

"Someone will see us," Billie said, rising slowly.

"I checked things over good before coming into
the village," Roy said. "The women and children are

too preoccupied to realize that something is happening to their chief's wife."

"After I sign the papers, what will you do with me?" Billie said, her pregnancy evident to Roy when she stood up, her round belly showing under her doeskin dress.

"And so now there's to be a baby from the savage?" Roy said, staring at her stomach. He grinned crookedly. "Well, *Mommy,* that won't stop me. Come on. I've wasted enough time talkin' to you."

Billie grabbed her sealskin cloak and secured it around her shoulders, then left the house with Roy. She saw no one, which meant that Roy had free rein to take her without anyone knowing. She had no choice but to cooperate.

He told her that he would let her go after she signed papers. But what would he do when he saw that the mansion was occupied by children?

Billie went to the stable and saddled her strawberry roan. Roy mounted his steed as Billie mounted hers.

"Now come on. I know your husband is felling trees. I know the best route to take so that he won't see us," Roy ordered.

"And that route is?" Billie asked, riding alongside him as they left the village and entered the forest.

"Exactly where they never ever cut because it's land that's not legally theirs," Roy said, smiling wickedly at her. "We'll take that roundabout way to get to the mansion. It's longer, but safer."

Billie smiled to herself, for that particular area was exactly where her husband was cutting today. With her father and the others gone, Proud Eagle and his men had gone on land that had once been her father's but was now hers. She had given all her land over to the Makah.

"It'll be over soon," Roy said, as they rode. "I won't kill you. All's I want are those papers signed over to me. Then you can go your way and I'll go mine."

"Sounds like a good plan to me," Billie said, giving him a sly smile. "All I want is to get through this without causing trauma to my baby. Let's get this behind us, Roy."

Soon he would discover that he was a fool for trying to get anything back. She was riding him into a trap.

Suddenly Roy drew a tight rein and stopped. He looked over at Billie. "You tricked me," he said tightly. "You've didn't tell me . . ."

He didn't say anything else. He had brought himself directly into the face of danger. He could hear the Makah lumberjacks busy at work, as their sounds echoed through the trees.

"You witch!" he said between clenched teeth. He didn't take time to draw his rifle and kill her. All he could think about was getting as far away from there as quickly as he could, or . . .

Billie sank her heels into the flanks of her steed

and rode hard in the direction of the sounds of a tree falling hard on the ground.

She opened her mouth to shout for Proud Eagle, but instead brought her horse to a sudden halt when she heard the pop of gunfire behind her.

She wheeled around and grew pale as she gazed in that direction, knowing that was where Roy had taken his path of escape.

Had Roy shot Proud Eagle?

Or . . . ?

She sighed with intense relief as Proud Eagle appeared through a break in the trees, his rifle smoking.

"Proud Eagle!" she cried, galloping toward him.

When he met her halfway, they stopped alongside each other. "He's dead," he said, reaching over and gently touching her face. "My wife, the evil man is finally dead. He rode directly into the area where we were cutting."

"I knew that he would," Billie said, tears filling her eyes.

Billie suddenly clutched her stomach.

"What is it?" Proud Eagle asked.

"I haven't felt all that well today," she said, dizzy again. "That's why I was alone in our longhouse. I—I didn't join the women. That's how Roy was able to come in and force me to leave with him. No one was outside where they could see him. The women . . . they . . . were in the council house, sewing and making their baskets."

She grabbed her head. "I'm so dizzy," she said, then flinched when a pain swept through her belly. "Proud Eagle, I need to go home. I need to have Blue Cloud check things. I am so afraid that I'm not going to be able to carry our baby to full term."

"Come with me," he said, looking over his shoulder as one of his men came in sight with Roy's body draped over the back of his horse.

"Lord, there he is," Billie said, paling at the sight.

She looked quickly away even though she was relieved that he could never cause her or her family another moment of trouble.

She rode with Proud Eagle back to the village, then went to the shaman's longhouse, where he quickly checked her.

When he was done, he smiled at Billie. "You are still carrying a healthy child," he said. "But it will be best if you spend more time in bed."

Billie was relieved that things seemed all right after all. "I will absolutely do as you say. I want this baby to stay healthy."

Proud Eagle walked with her to their longhouse and to her bed. She frowned. "If I'm to spend so much time in bed, I will be too shut away in here," she said. "I would rather have a pallet by the fire in the outer room. It calms me so to be able to gaze into the flames while resting."

"You shall have anything you want when you want it," Proud Eagle said, helping her back to the living room.

She sat in the rocking chair as he prepared a comfortable pallet of furs and blankets for her. He helped her down onto it, then lay beside her as they gazed together into the flames.

"This was a good day," he said, smiling at her.

"I might question that," Billie said, laughing softly.

"It was a good day in that Roy is finally gone out of our lives forever and in that our baby is all right," Proud Eagle said. He turned on his side and gently touched her belly. "Yes, it is a good day, my wife. We have so much to be thankful for."

"Yes, so much," Billie said, brushing away all thoughts of those terrible moments with Roy.

Finally, he was gone.

Epilogue

Three years had passed since that day when Roy had finally been wiped from Billie's life.

She and Proud Eagle were the happy parents of two sweet children. One a girl, the other a boy. The girl had been born first, and Billie couldn't be more content. Her family's lives were filled with much love and adoration, as were the lives of the Makah filled with a peace that their chief assured them by his leadership.

Billie was in her longhouse, making a blanket from dog hair. She had cleaned the fleece by beating in a special chalky white earth that removed the oil from the wool. To spin this wool, the women first twisted it into loose strands, then twisted the strands into yarn with a hand spindle.

Billie was weaving on a vertical loom that had been set up in her outer room. She deftly passed yarn in and out among warp threads that were held apart by wooden swords. Swords also were used to press weft threads firmly in place.

Billie's blanket was going to be even softer because she had mixed cattail fluff in with the wool dog fleece.

While Billie continued working, she smiled and gazed at Snow as he lay shorn of his thick coat. He had made his contribution to the blankets being made throughout the Makah homes.

"Snow, you look so pitiful," Billie said, as he looked sorrowfully at her. "But my hair grew back, and so shall your fur."

Yes, finally her hair had grown long enough for her to wear it as one long braid down her back.

When she heard soft whimpers, she gazed down the corridor where both her children were napping. Her daughter, Soft Wings, napped without stirring, but her young son, Proud Wings, always whimpered as he slept, even though nothing was ever visibly wrong to cause it.

Even so, she never hesitated to go and check on him. She hurried into the room where his cradle sat close to his sister's.

"Just look at you," Billie whispered as she reached down and touched his soft copper face. "You look so much like your father."

Seeing that he was all right, she tiptoed over to the other cradle, where her daughter was sleeping soundly. "And so do you," she whispered, admiring the baby's copper skin and the coal-black hair that had already grown down to her shoulders. "You are so beautiful."

"And so are you."

At Proud Eagle's voice behind her Billie turned quickly.

When he stepped up to her and swept his arms around her waist, drawing her close, she smiled sweetly up at him.

"And so you are through cutting trees today?" she asked in a hushed voice so as not to disturb the children's sleep.

"Yes, and I dropped in at the school to see how the children were doing," he said. "Many Winds caught me watching him from the door. But he did not mind. He smiled and waved."

"And was all well at the school?" Billie asked. She was very proud that things were going so well there.

"Seems Sara can't stay out of the kitchen," Proud Eagle said, chuckling. "It was snickerdoodle day again today. The children adore her cookie breaks."

"As did I," Billie said.

They went into the living room and stood before the fire.

Billie turned to Proud Eagle. "I am so content," she murmured. "And I see in your eyes that you share the same feeling."

"How could I not be content with you as my wife and with our three children to share our evenings with?" Proud Eagle said. He brushed soft kisses across her brow. "And our people? Never have I seen them as happy."

"Yes, I have seen it, too," Billie said. "I only pray

that no one else will come and disturb our happiness, our peace."

"Even if they do, we will be all right," Proud Eagle said. "As a people, as a tribe, we are strong and we have the tenacity to endure."

He took her hand and walked with her to the open door. They stepped outside and gazed at the Makah people, busy with their evening chores.

"My wife, our culture, our heritage, will carry us through any and all storms that our people face, today, tomorrow, and in the future," he said.

He led her back inside and pulled her into his arms. "As will our love for one another carry us through any storms that we might sometimes face," he said huskily.

"Yes, our love . . ." Billie whispered as his lips came down upon hers with a kiss.

"My husband," she whispered against his lips. "I believe we have time to share something more than talk. Don't you?"

He smiled down at her as he led her to their bed. "Yes, my wife, I do believe we have time for ourselves before our children awaken for their feeding," he said, already disrobing her.

Billie sighed as their naked bodies came together.

Letter to the Reader

Dear Reader:

I hope you enjoyed *Proud Eagle*. The next book in my Signet Indian series, which I am writing exclusively for NAL, will be *Silver Feather*, about the great and noble Choctaw Indians.

This book is filled with excitement, romance, and adventure. *Silver Feather* will be in the stores in June 2005.

Many of you say that you are collecting my Indian romances. For my entire backlist of books, for information about how to acquire the books that you cannot find, and for an autographed bookmark, my latest newsletter, and fan club information, please send a stamped, self-addressed legal-size envelope to:

CASSIE EDWARDS
6709 North Country Club Road
Mattoon, IL 61938

Thank you for your support of my Indian series. I love researching and writing about our country's beloved Native Americans, the very first, true people of our great, proud land.

Cassie Edwards